MW00681805

Way Up

WAY UP

stories

Kathryn Kuitenbrouwer

Kathryn Kuitenbrouwer

For Jeananne
Enjoy! with best
regards,
Kathy

GOOSE LANE

Copyright © Kathryn Kuitenbrouwer, 2003.

All rights reserved. No part of this work may be reproduced or used in any
form or by any means, electronic or mechanical, including photocopying,
recording, or any retrieval system, without the prior written permission of
the publisher or a licence from the Canadian Copyright Licensing
Agency (Access Copyright). To contact Access Copyright, visit
www.accesscopyright.ca or call 1-800-893-5777.

Edited by Laurel Boone.
Cover photograph: "Tall Self" ©Alan Babbitt Fine Art Photography,
www.abproductions.com.
Cover and interior design by Julie Scriver.
Printed in Canada by Transcontinental.
10 9 8 7 6 5 4 3 2 1

National Library of Canada Cataloguing in Publication

Kuitenbrouwer, Kathryn, 1965-
Way up / Kathryn Kuitenbrouwer.

Short stories.
ISBN 0-86492-368-6

I. Title.
PS8571.U4W39 2003   C813'.6   C2003-904198-0

Published with the financial support of the Canada Council for the Arts,
the Government of Canada through the Book Publishing Industry
Development Program, and the New Brunswick Culture
and Sports Secretariat.

Goose Lane Editions
469 King Street
Fredericton, New Brunswick
CANADA E3B 1E5
www.gooselane.com

To Marc

Contents

11 The Nez Perce Ride Again

25 What Had Become of Us

43 Way Up

57 The Vastness of the Lie

65 The Burial

85 The Mortification of Frances Brady

93 The End of the Line

107 Dead Man's Sheets

125 Blue Skinned Potatoes

131 Falling Out

151 Martha's Stint with the IRA

163 Batterie Todt

179 The Last Magic Forest

Acknowledgements

I would like to express my gratitude to the Ontario Arts Council for financial support during the writing of many of these stories. I am very grateful to my editor, Laurel Boone, and to Susanne Alexander, both of Goose Lane Editions. I would like to thank Hilary McMahon and Westwood Creative Artists for their support of my work.

Stories from this book have appeared in *Descant*, *Prairie Fire*, *Blood & Aphorisms*, *Prism International* and *Smoke*. In the story "What Had Become of Us," the lines "I piss like before in the sink / I sleep with my clothes on / what a lousy life" are my translation from Bram Vermeulen's song "Rode Wijn." I am thankful for the early support of Don Summerhayes, Merlin Homer, George Murray and Ailsa Craig. I would like to thank my husband, Marc Kuitenbrouwer, and our sons, Linden, Jonas and Christopher, for their general patience and respect for my dream-seeking. Steven Naylor and Holly Farrell are steadfast critics, to whom I am ever grateful. Thank you, also, to Dawne McFarlane, Deirdre Meyer, Christine Fischer-Guy, Lorna McFee, Melanie Noviss, and my mother, Ann Walsh. A special thanks to my dad, Bryan Walsh, upon whose suggestion I "put more sex in."

The Nez Perce Ride Again

My dad's a gimp, you know; one leg's shorter than the other and atrophied from the knee down, from the polio. It doesn't stop him. It drives him. The horse he boarded on our farm that fall was a big, sturdy Appaloosa stallion named Abel. He was a gentle but high-spirited horse, subdued only by the nasty pus-dribbling and swollen injury on his front left pectoral muscle. He'd been kicked regularly by an ill-tempered pack horse that ran with a local Appaloosa herd. The herd owner was a woman horse breeder by the name of Moira, who lived well east of our farm. She was boxy in shape and curt as hell.

No one rides the horse, she said. I'll come by early spring to fetch it. 'Spect by then that wound'll be healed.

She paid for the full winter's board by cheque. Then she hoisted herself up into the cab of her GMC, ground the gears, and drove out in reverse.

Goddamn horse is trying to lie on me, Dad called. He was inside the trailer, preparing to get the Appaloosa out. Horses don't much like walking backwards. I could hear Dad grunting and see the trailer swaying, could tell from his voice he didn't mind it one bit. There's a reason he was boarding the Appaloosa besides the bare obvious. I'll get to it.

Ma! he called to Nana. Will you get Pauline and Bonnie out of the way, now. Damn horse. Nana lived with us and minded us when Mum was at work.

Nana said, You okay, Gerard?

Yeah. Just wisht this horse'd back out.

Abel rubbed his butt against the rusted frame of the trailer and backed out slowly, shifting his buttocks, swinging his enormous earth-touching cock. We girls sucked in breath.

What's that? I asked.

It's a horse. An Appaloosa.

No. That. What's that?

Shh.

It looks like lipstick.

Shh.

The horse dwarfed my father. It gave him the appearance of being even shorter than he was. Nana always maintained that he would have been a tall man if only he had not been stricken with infantile paralysis at the age of eight. She claimed he was unnaturally, ungenetically short, shorter than any man on either side had ever been within living memory, and that he would most assuredly have been a six-footer if not for the disease. The polio had withered him right down.

Dad had overcome, though, practised normalizing his gait, so that his walk took on a rolling, vaguely bouncy lilt. People who did not know wondered whether this springiness was a mannerism certain short men develop to give the appearance of status. Some said his shortness betrayed a mental shortcoming, an inferiority complex. But this could not have been further from the truth. My father, who regarded his measured height, five feet four inches, with complacency, had a certain inner tallness that more than compensated for what God's hand had wrought; he was an assured, quietly ambitious man who looked forward.

Keep back, girls, he said. He was leading Abel, pulling strong at the lead rope to slow him down, to the corral gate. Abel sashayed for a piece, hooves prancing high, and then he dug in, pawing at the gravel. The Appaloosa's cock swung up to touch his underbelly, sloshing jism along the ground. Dad yanked violently on the rope in a way that worried me, like he would get mad and do something. But the horse acquiesced and was happy he had. Dad unhooked the lead and nudged him free into the corral.

My dad was eight when Nana scolded him for walking funny down the stairs.

Stop being so silly! she said.

When he fell in a lump and tumbled down to the landing, she realized her error. Dad was in hospital with polio for months. He lay helpless on a rigid plank hospital bed. And as he recuperated, he spent his time reading. He ordered books by topic. Nana visited him every day there, bringing home-baked snacks made from recipes out of Fanny Merrit Farmer's *Food and Cookery for the Sick and Convalescent*: Invalid Muffins, Coddled Egg, Marshmallow Pudding. And she brought books from the library, a small stack every day or two. He ate all of it up. He'd never, never talk about it; it's my nana told me this.

Dad had an appetite for books about Indians, so Nana borrowed for him every book on tribal lore and Indian history that could be had. He loved reading up on Wounded Knee and the Iroquois battles, but his all-time favourite stories revolved around Chief Joseph and the Nez Perce tribe. I found one of his old books on that in a cardboard box in the basement, ex libris, a lucky find, I suppose. The Nez Perce bred the original Appaloosas. They were a wealthy tribe before their land was stolen from them by bad treaties and politicians bent on providing land for voting citizens. This came to a head when some hotheaded young warriors took revenge by murdering a couple of rowdy homesteaders. Chief Joseph gathered his people and tried to flee. The cavalry was given shooting orders, but the Nez Perce realized they were not just fighting for their lives but also for their beautiful, fertile Wallowa Valley, their culture.

For three months, they fought. They crossed seventeen hundred miles and three states, pressing their herd of two thousand spotted horses through country that was treacherous both geographically and tactically in a vain attempt to reach sanctuary in Canada. The Nez Perce had no Indian allies by the time of their defeat.

The citizens of the United States were terrified of them, and the other Indian nations saw no benefit in such a dangerous liaison. Proud Chief Joseph laid down his arms and famously "fought no more forever" forty miles from the Canadian border. The American cavalry dispersed, stole or shot whatever horses they found.

Dad's plan was to winter the Appaloosa out of doors. He felt that the cold and the freedom would heal the wound. There was plenty of forested shelter, several salt licks and the company of two boarder mares and a Palomino pony that belonged to Pauline, my younger sister. Abel could find grain, hay and water at the barn. If the bathtub trough froze over, the horses slaked their thirst by eating snow.

The Appaloosa whinnied, reared up, front hooves jabbing at the air, and then galloped recklessly, tossing his mane and tail. The bay, the quarter horse and the little Palomino looked on, nonplussed. Over the next few days, the Appaloosa tried to mount them all, even the pony, which bucked and screeched plaintively.

He'll calm down, Ma.

He's brutalizing that bay horse.

He'll settle in.

He did not. Abel chewed at the fencing and kicked dirt. When Dad brought the pony out for Pauline and me to ride, the Appaloosa stretched his neck through the upper two rungs of the fence, retracted his lips and tried to nip. He whinnied forlornly and rolled his strangely human eyes as we rode the pony back and forth along the path between the corral and the old pigsty.

Abel's crying, I said.

Horses can't cry, Bonnie.

Abel can, Daddy.

The horse was healing slowly. The infection had drained, but the scabby sore kept ripping open. He rubbed his foreleg against the gate whenever we rode the Palomino, scratched at the wound relentlessly. Dad would get into the corral most weekends to groom him. He brought a footstool to give him the height he needed to brush Abel's withers and mane properly. He brushed that horse for hours, doctored the sore with ointment from the vet and let Abel nuzzle him, searching for carrots. The horse snuffled the carrots out of Dad's hand, pulled back his lips and grinned his yellow-brown buckteeth at us. When Dad walked away, Abel waited until he was almost to the gate and then came tearing after him, stampeding, then veering off at the last possible second. Dad never turned around. That horse and he always had a special connection.

When my father healed well enough to go back to school, he discovered that where he'd been popular the year before, now he was a pariah. Even those whose friendship he thought he could count on, true chums and bosom buddies of the previous year, had been instructed not to play with him. The poor boy was an invalid, disabled and most likely enfeebled entirely. He was teased mercilessly. The children called him names — bandy-leg, cripple, crip, lame, weak-knee, even wounded knee, which, of course, gave him immense pleasure. There were nicknames and insults he would never divulge to Nana, they were that unspeakable. The schoolchildren tripped him at every opportunity; their laughter rang echoing through the hallways.

Dad looked up the word invalid in the dictionary and laughed. Scoffing didn't get him friends, though. And so, since no one would play with him and he stood at recess all alone, the world looked different. It took on a frenzied noisiness that vaguely embarrassed him. He withdrew, became studious, focused on mathematics and skipped two grades. This gave him the notoriety of genius, a moniker that was either one rung up or one rung down the social ladder from leper, depending on who was asked. The Appaloosa horse became, for Dad, the emblem of the Nez Perce's tenacity. And Abel was that dream horse incarnate, the great equalizer. Dad's handicap would rest inconsequentially upon him. Together they could traverse the Plains as one — one whole.

That horse wants to be ridden, my father said to the air one night at dinner.

Mum gave him a warning look.

It'd calm him down.

You'll lose the board if you ride him.

That horse is frantic for riding, Annie.

The Appaloosa was frantic for something. He had his cock out more often than not, a detail that was intensely fascinating to Pauline and me. We were both nine. Pauline was exactly ten months younger than me, so that, for two months every year, we were peers, barely one gestation apart, Irish twins. We watched as Dad rubbed Abel's speckled coat down, watched as Abel sent his penis lower and lower to the ground in gratitude for all the attention. The cock was thick and dappled, with a pink knobby end that arched vaguely back up. Abel could whip it up to his body, but he hardly ever did that. He just let it hang lazily down. We code-named that dick "lipstick," and Pauline taught me everything I might ever need to know about it.

Look. Lipstick, Bonnie, lipstick.

What's it for?

Mum told me it's for peeing, Pauline said.

Really?

It's a lie. It's for doing it.

It?

Pauline told me in fine detail how the reproductive system worked. She leaned into me conspiratorially, nodded to the upstairs master bedroom window.

They're probably doing it right now, she whispered.

I started crying.

It's true. He sticks his huge lipstick in her. I'm sure she hates it.

I looked through my blurry eyes at Abel's cock, and I didn't believe a word of it, even though I knew it was so audacious it must be true. That's what all that jumping up on the other horses was about. It was ridiculous.

Do you know for sure she hates it? I asked.

Well, it must hurt. It must.

Maybe Dad's is smaller.

Bonnie, it must reach his nose.

I gasped and shook my head.

Yes, Bonnie.

Abel came up and leaned over the fence, beckoning us. I came to him and he nuzzled my arm, snorting affectionately. He laid his head on my shoulder and eyed me humanly, his sclera full of compassion. There was something beseeching about that animal.

When he was a boy, Nana told me, my father played seriously and privately and seldom, and when he did, he played Cowboys and Indians in the back yard with his younger brother, Evan. Dad fashioned a bow out of a branch torn from a yew shrub in the local park and made long, pointy arrows from deadfall twigs. To these he fastened feathers culled from a pigeon corpse he found. An aunt had brought him a headdress while he was recuperating, a real but simple one purchased at Niagara Falls. Later, he made a little tomahawk and played at being Chief Joseph. He fought relentlessly with Evan, wrestling him, mock scalping him, yipping in triumph. But Evan was a tireless opponent, and it didn't matter how often he succumbed to the knife, he always sought revenge. Evan, with his bashed-in felt cowboy hat and bright red suede vest, his rusted, dented six-guns holstered in his jeans pockets, eventually cornered his slow-moving older brother.

Stick 'em up, dirty redman.

And my dad turned, dropped his weapons and folded his arms.

I will fight no more forever.

Whereupon Evan shot him through the heart and, nobly, he died.

Chief Joseph had never scalped anyone in his life, nor had he died of gunshot when he surrendered. Over six feet tall, he was a pacifist, desperately trying to avoid war, resolute in his conviction that his father had not sold Nez Perce land. He didn't want bloodshed but he didn't want to lose his homeland, the sacred tribal burial ground or the Appaloosa herd.

Abel may have been the manifestation of my dad's childhood fascination, the realization of certain boyish dreams, but to Pauline and me he was a constant source of sexual speculation. One night in the cool, still, autumn darkness, Pauline hissed at me from the lower bunk in our room, Bonnie! Come down.

Why?

Just come.

I crawled under the comforter with my sister. She said, shh, shh, and pulled up my nightgown. Hers was already hitched to her chest.

Shh, shh.

She lay on top of me, our soft baby genitals touching. She lay very still for a long time. Then she started humping me with her buttocks. I had seen some of the barn cats linked together, spasming. She humped and thumped on me faster and harder. I lay still. I didn't move. She was grinding into me so hard it hurt.

This is what it's like, she said. This is how you have to do it.

How do you know?

Suzie Damer showed me.

You shouldn't sleep over there.

I know. I think her brother taught her.

Eeww, yuck.

I know.

Pauline held me like a precious cup. It was the secrecy we savoured. It displaced us from childishness. We shared in adulthood but without the adults knowing, and that one detail held enormous power. We felt we knew everything, our secret held all knowledge; youth and silence were the perfect cover.

We drew horses. I was the better artist, rendering them from various skewed perspectives, sometimes in small herds. I worked the sketches in crayon and watercolour, occasionally setting up my easel outside and trying to sell my work. I had hundreds of horse-head details on small scraps of paper, which I sold to Dad and Mum and Nana for a nickel apiece. Pauline's drawings were cartoonish, somewhat base and top secret. Her horses had visible vaginas and penises that reached their mouths. The pictures had captions that read, Neigh! or Yummy! Sometimes the genitals had captions. The best was a caricature of the Appaloosa, his cock wrapping his body lengthwise, its tip fashioned into a microphone but spilling little dashes of urine, and the caption bubble read, Testing, one, two, pee. This had to be hidden away. I bought it from her for a steep dime and locked it in my diary.

We humped each other regularly. When the evening stilled, Pauline would climb up or I down, we would furtively kiss with open mouths. These were studied romantic kisses that we practised less for sensation than appearance. Pauline and I wanted to look good kissing with the princes we imagined for later. Sometimes we rubbed ourselves together, feeling each other up. We sought inspiration from Harold Robbins novels smuggled from the municipal library. I added romantic gestures to the game. I left wildflowers under Pauline's pillow. She replied with a braided strand of horsehair. We poked Mum's sewing needles into our fingers and bled into each other, making a solemn pact.

I will not tell upon pain of excruciating death, I swore.

I will not tell on pain of having my eyeballs removed and eaten by pygmy cannibals. Pauline looked at me wildly and added, I'd die if you told.

Me too, I said.

The lovemaking experiments lasted into the winter, at which point I abruptly stopped them. Pauline would call me to her bed and I would pretend to be asleep. I realize now that I may have hurt my sister by ignoring her and that I had broken our pact by not letting her into my confidence. I'm sorry for that. The fact was, by my tenth birthday, in the dead of winter, I had a new secret that shifted the balance of my relationship with Pauline.

Abel had begun to grow fond of me. He would come to rest his head on me over the fence. I looked into the cool, lovely whites of his eyes, and I realized he was not displaying compassion at all but plaintively begging, willing me, pleading with me to ride him. I petted him under his forelock and muttered encouraging words to him. Abel crouched on his front legs, beckoning me to climb on him.

Why can't we ride Abel, Dad?

Dad said, Horse breeders are all crazy.

But he wants me to ride on him. He crouched like a circus horse for me.

If she cared about him at all, she'd at least come and ride him herself.

I'd love to ride Abel. Think how fast we'd go.

Yeah, horse breeders are nuts.

I decided instead to dress the Palomino. I groomed and braided her tail and mane, weaving blue and pink ribbon in here and there. I dragged out Dad's old sulky, found the ancient dung-encrusted heavy horse harness in the stable and draped it over the pony, fitting it as best I could with no real experience of how these things worked. I adorned the pony with large, jangling sledding bells. She looked marvellous. Just as I was about to manoeuvre myself onto the seat of the sulky, however, the pony suddenly flared her nostrils and pinned back her ears. She lunged and bucked and tore to and fro across the lawn and down into the dry bed creek, splintering the chariot to shards, losing the harness and eventually finding sanctuary deep in the cedar bush.

Dad did not scold as we quietly doctored the pony's injuries and then went about the property picking up the debris.

Are you all right, Bonnie? he asked.

Yes.

It was too heavy, I guess.

I guess.

Full winter came soon after. The snow fell leisurely all day and all night for weeks. Christmas and my birthday came and went. The snow fell and fell. It hushed the world and insulated it and slowed everything down except the Appaloosa, which took vast pleasure in rolling and galloping through the drifts that formed like dunes in the corral. Dad took the quarter horse riding along a broken path through the bush and the network of hayfields. I rode behind him on the bay horse, for she was the most docile and predictable. Abel became violently jealous, whinnying and braying so loudly that we could still hear him at the back of the fifty-acre property. This grieved Dad so much he decided to go back, bridle Abel and bring him along. The Appaloosa took the bit hungrily.

Couldn't we, just this once? I asked.

The owner said no.

It's silly. No one will see.

It's the owner who pays. It's the owner who says. Dad made it rhyme for a joke.

But he clearly hated it. An unridden horse was a waste for all parties. He threw a woollen blanket over Abel's back and loins to keep the heat in as we trotted. But the steed had no intention of trotting. As soon as he reached an open field, he gave in to instinct, reared and bolted, ripping the bridle out of my father's hands and tearing down the pasture, blanket flying.

Goddamn. Dad cupped his leather-burned hand.

We would have to race to catch up. The bay was lazy, and I couldn't nudge her past a fast trot. I tried to post, but the horse had an awkward gait that kept sending me into an eye-bouncing jiggle. By the time we reached the frozen creek, Abel was nowhere to be seen, even if I could have focused.

Dad yelled over to me, You go that-a-way, and I'll go this-a-way.

I laughed and spurred my indolent steed on and on. The back field was fallow, grown up with pussy willows and alders. It was frozen swampland and difficult to navigate. There were groundhog holes to avoid; I had to keep my eyes on the path even while searching for Abel. I saw the steam rising off him before I could make out his form. He looked sideways at me and pawed the turf, breaking through the ice in jabs that sounded like glass breaking. He nodded at me and grinned his yellow bucked smile, lowered onto his knees and extended his head to the ground in compliance.

I'll catch hell, I said to him. Abel shifted his head, human eye shining.

I dismounted my horse, threw the reins around a prickly shrub, and walked slowly to Abel. I patted and rubbed his back, and then, slowly, I swung my leg over him and leaned into his neck. The Appaloosa whinnied triumphantly.

Stay still, stay, I whispered, I prayed. And the horse stayed. He lifted his head and whinnied still louder and snorted, sniffing the breeze. He knew everything about the fallow field, every hibernating mouse, every dormant pupa. Horse sense. He certainly knew the whereabouts of my dad, struggling through the undergrowth toward us. The quarter horse had obstinately refused to pass an enormous slab of granite that had heaved out of the ground and sprouted its own small forest. Spooked and unreasonable, the horse was abandoned where it stalled.

Dad seemed to appear magically. I had not heard him approach nor thought to listen for him. Once on Abel, I had all I could do not to spur him to action. I sobered when Dad's form broke through the brush. My apologetic face could not have been more genuinely feigned.

I'm sorry, I muttered.

Dad looked up at me on that eager horse and laughed a gut laugh you rarely hear in adults. Its giddiness thrilled through me. We did not talk. We did not make a blood pact or swear secrecy.

Go, he said, and waved his hand.

Abel swung his head and kicked up snow. He trotted in a zigzag through the brush, across the frozen field until he found solid ground. He broke first into a controlled canter and then began to gallop. Then he raced full speed across the field so that to stay on, I laid my torso along his mane and held him around the neck. Abel moved so fast and with such other-worldly grace that I cannot remember the feel of the horse's form beneath me but only the wind catching in my throat and the cold slamming my face as I flew.

When it was over, I stood between the bay and the quarter horse that my father had rescued from the back field, and I watched as Dad mounted the exhilarated Appaloosa. He twitched Abel's rump with the rein, and they receded so fast into the distance they might as well have vanished. I stood and listened to my heart racing from the pure speed of the experience, and then I grabbed the reins that dangled from the horses on either side of me, and I slowly walked back home.

Pauline was the first to see me. She came running up, wide-eyed.

Where's Dad?

Mum ran out to the stable when she saw me bring the horses in for their brush-down. I donned my best nonchalant look, a queer mirror to my mother's natural and unabashed anxiety.

Where's your father? Is he hurt? Where is he?

Don't worry, I said. It's just Abel. Abel's broken free.

I tried to be convincing, to keep my face straight and sober, to ignore the shrill and distant Indian yelps that sang on the chill winter air, my dad's voice joyously yippee-yiy-yaying deep in the back fifty.

What Had Become of Us

Pieter Van Dongen and I were in another forest completely, and not surprisingly, my life had changed irrevocably and in subtle ways that I did not necessarily wish to examine. The acknowledging of change in any way brought with it a tenderness, a weepiness, a general atmosphere of misery that I would sooner deny. The forest in which we stood had been ravaged by a hurricane. Very few trees had survived the winds. It was a year to the day since Erwin's death.

What are we supposed to do here? I asked.

Cleaning up, Pieter said.

I had come to Belgium in order to leave Canada. It was as simple and as complicated as that could be. I wanted to leave home, family — a family I suspected of subversive politeness and congeniality, which was okay if you liked that sort of thing, but I had decided that on the whole I didn't — and seek the sort of autonomy that I expected might be found in the arms of a foreigner, on foreign terrain, in the imagined, nuanced otherness of a stranger's bed, in heavily accented intercourse. I had dreams — vivid sleeping dreams — that assured me this was possible, and so I sought, in my naivety, a non-Canadian boyfriend, a saviour from a far-off land, someone cultivated, if possible, but certainly non-English speaking. I had no desire for argument.

I met Pieter in a dingy university bar in the oldest section of

Ghent. It was full of miserable intellectuals for the most part, people who snorted instead of laughed, as if they were entirely above humour. He was different, of course, else I'd never have bothered with him. He was all gangly and confident. He had a small logging operation. It was hard to imagine anyone logging in Belgium, and so I found him generally amusing, archaic; I suppose I fell in love with him almost immediately. He spoke a disjointed, dysfunctional English, which made everything he said sound charming and vaguely stupefied.

You like me. I like you. We are aliking each other, he said. Is this good?

Do you hire women on your logging crews? I asked this demurely and out of pure tactic. We were standing beside each other at the bar, drinking blanchkes with little peels of lemon sinking down into them. It was obvious I was having him on; I was a terrible flirt. Of course, I was over there with only one goal in mind. I could be very stubborn, a real stickler for goals and such. He was adorable, all standing-up hair and questioning eyes, clean-shaven. He stared at me, not understanding the question.

I repeated, Do you ever have women working for you?

Oh, no, never, he said.

Really? I'm very strong.

Yes, oh, I would hire you, Adriana. This is special.

That was how it started. An enormous amount of time had passed since. Pieter's English had come to be letter perfect; I had come to see that the goal of autonomy was a shifting bastard of a thing. That ideal of self, a container of you-ness or me-ness, was a facile improbability, as all ideals are. I was not unhappy; I was hurtling toward happiness at all times. I had attained some sort of freedom — the sort given by your loved ones even as they cleave to you. Maybe that's all a person could expect.

I wished I had slept with Erwin before he died, before Pieter felled the spindly little scrap of a tree that would decapitate him and end his days on earth. They were brothers, you know. I wish I had the pleasure and misery of certain memories of Erwin's hand along the inside of my thigh, the surfacing of orgasm like a shattering of any possibility. I could languish in the grudge that the widow bears the dead and the almost-faux secret the adulteress coddles from her husband (for he must know, he must). My miscreant behaviour would not have been against Pieter. I would have slept with Erwin in spite of my love for Pieter, in spite of myself and all common sense, in spite of Erwin, who no doubt would have had his own good reasons for not crossing the line, yet could not, just as I could not, forestall the fates.

The poplar trees in this mess of a forest all these years later had been planted in 1946 under the instruction of the Belgian government, once the ash from the Second World War had settled. The distance between each of these trees, the distance between all trees in Belgium, was set at eight metres. The undergrowth was grassy where it wasn't overgrown with stinging nettle or damped down by rotting leaves. A recent hurricane had spun the tops of the trees viciously in twisted circles and back on themselves, plucked them out of the earth like so many weeds and thrown them down like little sticks on top of each other. Their trunks flexed unnaturally; some of these trees were thirty metres in height (now length), and the torque build-up in their stems was enormously dangerous if you happened to want to try to trim the branches, cut the roots away, clean the butt end and chop the leaders off, which is exactly what we intended to do. We expected the trees to violently resist our taming.

This one's for Erwin, Pieter said. He dedicated every forest he felled or cleaned up to his brother, as if an accumulation of offerings would alter the course of history. I watched the chimney stack of the Doem nuclear station off to the left, far in the distance, its smoke billowing in a cumulus of waste and condensation. The infrastructure for the building was largely underground; the stack was huge. They were having problems with fish — herring mostly — being drawn into the reactor by the tens of thousands. They were drawn through the water intake into the heavy water tanks. Pieter and Erwin used to slide herring down their throats, whole.

These are fantastic, Adriana. Open up.

Yes, open up, Erwin had said, forcing me to sit and then pulling my head back, making me laugh so that he could bring a fish down over my tongue. I gagged on the salty ocean meat; he held his open palm along my throat.

Hollanders and the people of the lowlands have a great love for herring. They smoke by the millions those caught off the coast in the cold currents of the North Sea, and what is more, they pickle the rest and can them in attractive little aluminum tins, the lids of which peel off with the help of a sort of Allen key. They stand at market, and have done so for centuries, in little manly groups, tilting their heads back and sliding the fish down their gullets. It is a tradition — men in wooden clompen and blue marine sweaters (knitted in cables and tied with effeminate pompoms at the neck), their throats translucently white, like swans swallowing. The Doem laboratories subcontracted the job, installing underwater screens and noisemakers to keep the herring in safe water. A loud, dull, unfriendly din was broadcast beneath the sea, and still the herring were awed by the sucking intake toward the heavy water containers. Some slipped through the protective mesh. The rest huddled, their noses bumping again and again into the screen, listening to the whirr of eradication.

Pieter and Erwin had been singing a song, and when they finished, they rolled open a tin of little dead fishes and laughed at my disgust and slid them into their mouths. I felt Erwin's hand undulate along the shape of the fish, creating space in my esophagus; his fingertips ran slightly under my sweater. I could have left Pieter in our bed that night and gone to him — his hand would run down my throat, my hand would draw his foreskin down, we should kiss then, a line of spittle between our tongues.

Pieter had introduced me to Erwin within days of my arrival in Ghent.

He's better than me in every way.

Erwin was a tall, tousle-haired dirty blond with a cheeky smile and a lanky off-kilter walk, like an overgrown child. He was not better in any way than Pieter but rather was a sort of complement, as if the two brothers, so close in age, had taken only certain human aspects and nurtured them but left the rest to rot, knowing that the other would compensate. We ate together every night — we called these meals homemade primitives — stews or omelettes, spaghetti. Once we dumped osso bucco unceremoniously on the table, no plates or cutlery, salad scattered in the centre. We ate like that to alleviate the banality of life and because it made us laugh. We drank plonk directly out of the bottle and laughed and laughed.

Erwin's death precipitated a personality gap in Pieter, of course, a void which initially filled with sorrow. I believe that death became a strange life force in our relationship. The actions of our daily lives were a direct result of our sadness; we were affected, I say touched, by that ghost of loss.

He's not coming back, I said.

I don't expect it, either.

But you wish.

He said, There is a crooner song Erwin and I used to sing — I piss like before in the sink/ I sleep with my clothes on/ what a lousy life.

So, you don't even wish it.

It's like this, I think, he said as he sat down on a fallen tree trunk, which bounced like a park toy. I don't expect it, and I don't wish it. It's over. But still a part of me looks over my shoulder and recognizes him in other people, as if he has scattered — little atoms and molecules seeking a place in this stranger's hair colour, that one's glint of the eye. He has become a series of lost pieces.

I took a swig from Pieter's thermos. It was not coffee. The wine was bitter at first, its sweetness hidden within this cold unhappiness. I took comfort in Pieter, in his body — his handsome face which was vaguely flattened out, his high cheekbones; he was older in appearance than in reality. The muscles in his back extended up into his convex neck, giving his head a look of stability. His hair was golden in the diffused Flemish light. His lips had a curving sensuality. Weather had given his forehead a furrow of concern; he had an elegant body curving into natural muscles, his penis a fascinating exclamation mark.

He had been working the forests across Belgium for more than ten years. We sat quietly there on the lopped branch for some time beside a line of Stihl chainsaws, a can of oil, a can of gasoline. I wondered about it, about the atomic dispersal of Erwin. The arc of Pieter's penis, had it changed, shifted from left to right, lightened slightly in hue? There were still parts of his body unexplored. I made a mental note to slow down, take my time about it. A waft of gasoline blew past on the wind, sweet.

When's the crane supposed to be here?

By noon.

Do you have a plan?

It's going to be a day from hell, I can tell you.

As far as the eye could see, not a tree was left standing. The wreckage hung limp from upturned root systems or snapped right off. The jagged, splintered wood was a pale, sap-shiny yellow. I climbed down into a crater, the negative space where the roots of a tree had been. The earth beneath was muddy. I lifted my boots, pumped the squelching mess and enjoyed the sensation of suction resistance.

If you cut off the stem now, I'll be buried alive.

Come out.

Come in and see what it feels like.

No, Adriana.

I looked up into the gnarled mess of roots and earth. Larvae wriggled back in. Little shards of coloured glass, old detritus reflected the sun back at me.

Hey, look at this.

It's an old landfill, a dump, that's all.

Look, there's a road for little creatures here, along the roots and between them, coming up along the surface.

What do you see in these worms? Anything hopeful?

What could be more hopeful than death and decay? Do me a favour and cut off that damn stem. I won't feel a thing.

Pieter said, I have work to do.

The trees had swayed in the autumn breeze just one week before. The leaves had just begun to react to the lessening light, to turn yellow and brown and to fall. Small animals had hoarded food here. Children had played in this forest, screamed laughing, running away from imagined predation. Adults had nestled into the composting leaves and swayed to more primal necessities, in lieu of love. A forester had made the rounds, a shotgun slapping his green-corduroyed thigh, a spaniel at his side.

We'd been caught once, Pieter and I, in flagrante delicto, by the brindle hondt, the water dog that every forester seemed to own. The snuffling, cold snout had alerted us in time to hastily clothe ourselves and appear unflushed, deep into our lovemaking as we had been.

Goeie Morgen, the forester had said.

And to you, I replied.

You're English, he said.

Canadian.

Then he noticed and spluttered, Why, you're a girl!

I had flicked the switch on my Stihl 64 and pulled the cord; the machine roared to life. I nodded at him by way of excusing myself and got to work, using the chainsaw as a sort of machete, clearing the bramble and nettle from around the closest tree. I was wet between the legs. Pieter and I were in the bower of our love affair then, the first month. I cannot imagine making love out of doors now except as an act of pretense or desperation.

Lately, our lovemaking had taken on the sobriety of a Mass, of a wound healing; it was a communion of sadness. And we drew Erwin into even that. In the dampness of our bed, humid and hot, we talked of nothing else.

How could you, I mean, in that big forest, with all that space around. One man is so small.

I don't know how it happened.

You don't know?

It's a mess right now, Adriana. In my head. Did I do it on purpose without meaning to do it on purpose — fantasy out of control? A waking dream? I wish I had done it on purpose. It would make sense then.

Pieter, I wasn't suggesting that. I meant something about

probabilities. Space and motion and mathematics. The field was so big, the tree so small, that kind of thing.

I felled the tree into an empty space. Then, there he was.

Are you suggesting . . . ? I whispered even though there were only the two of us in the house.

Inconceivable, he said.

The tree that killed Erwin was not really worth chopping. At less than half a cubic meter of useable wood, it didn't look as if it could kill a fly. Erwin didn't see it coming, felt, as they say, not a thing. His life did not flash before his eyes, not that that's any consolation. He died instantly. Pieter shouted and ran, but it was too late. He held him, held him as if he could, like making a puzzle, reunite his body with his body. I was not there. I had taken the day off because my birthday was coming up and I wanted to have a day to myself. I had gone to purchase an album of Bulgarian vocal music. I had it on the turntable at top volume when Pieter came home, his hands bloodied, the tattered quilted workshirt he wore soaked through with Erwin's stuff; bits of brain matter and wood chips clung where the flannel shirt had worn through, the cotton insulation spilling out. The nuances of the Bulgarian's song, the layers of complex vocal arrangement were already forming into something unreliable, some memory we could try to grasp later to force sense out of the senseless.

You could have pushed the tree sideways.

I didn't . . . it didn't occur to me.

No. I just wondered. If he'd been just paralyzed . . .

He would have hated that.

We could wheel him around in a chair, I said. I thought about his helpless body, about undressing him, the heavy useless limbs, the limp curve of spine, like dead but not, just not.

With every tree he cut down, Pieter's body took on the shape of the stem. He leaned into his work in a kind of yearning posture. He rose as the tree passed its centre and began its fall. Then he shifted and stood and watched it fall, often pulling out his Drum tobacco to roll a cigarette even as the trunk crashed to earth. When the back of Erwin's skull broke away, when Pieter saw the brain was crushed and bits of bone had shattered like china into the mess of his brother, he did all he could. He acted pragmatically, picked up the cap of Erwin's skull and fitted it back as well as he could manage, unaware of the blood spillage. He nestled Erwin's head into his own lap, holding him together for some time, as if time would heal all wounds. Pieter kept his focus on Erwin's face; he claimed it took on an otherworldly beauty. He drew his hand over it and shut the glazed eyes. Then he stood up and in horror ran out of the forest in search of help.

I cut it perfectly. He wasn't there . . .

Then he was there?

. . . suddenly, out of nowhere.

I knew Pieter had the habit of checking the intended landing spot of each tree before he felled it. Once he waited for an hour to let a somnambulant hedgehog waddle out of danger's path. The tree that killed Erwin was destined to be left on the forest floor as compost. It had a parasitic ivy vining up its bark, rot running through the core. Pieter glanced over and waited for his brother to get out of the way, made an all clear sign and waited for one in return, and then he nestled his shoulder into the trunk and sliced through the last remaining hinge of wood. What he saw when he looked up was impossible. Time had reversed, mangled itself, for now Erwin was back in the way of the falling tree.

Pieter brought me to the place where Erwin had died. Together we found the inconsequential stump. It aggravated me that the tree was not bigger or of a more exotic species. It annoyed me that flowers dared bloom, flowers that Erwin would never see or smell. The stump had already begun its slow decay; the sap had risen and congealed into hard droplets. Erwin had been chemically embalmed, wrapped in plastic, his legs and arms broken to fit into a standard-size coffin. He had been mourned and buried deep in a sandy pit in the oldest working graveyard in the city. One day when I went to pay my respects, I fell, half intentionally, into a freshly dug grave near Erwin's tombstone. Deep in the ground, I grabbed to gain a hold along the edges, which only gave way, sprinkling my feet with sand and burying them. Pieter leaned over and laughed despite himself.

Going so soon? he said. Then, he jumped down with me into the grave. We lay down together in the bottom of the pit, our arms folded across our chests. We noticed artifacts of previous burials embedded in the walls, corroded metal crucifixes, a bashed set of dentures, little bones and shards of other bones, a necklace and a hearing aid. I climbed on Pieter's shoulders to get out of the pit and pulled him up until he could brace his knee on the earth's surface. The stone pathway out of the graveyard was an homage to those dead whose relatives could no longer afford the annual cemetery fee. The coffins had been dug up, the remains cremated, and the tombstones smashed and fashioned into a walkway. I skirted the inscriptions.

What could be more morbid than this? I asked Pieter.

It's just a practicality.

It's outrageous, bodies flung all over. Cats prowling everywhere.

Life goes on, Pieter said.

Even then, in the rawness of our loss, a transformation was taking place. The gap was closing in. We were quietly re-forming ourselves, nurturing aspects within ourselves and in each other that reminded us of Erwin. We were compensating, filling in the spaces he had occupied. Slowly, invisibly, he was returning to us by our sheer willingness to have him here.

I should have gone up to his room, with its unadorned simplicity — a waif walking naked through the damp chill and dark, willing the body warmth of my first bed to carry me to my second. I imagine the sex would have been rough and primal and seeking only the most primitive of human outlets, a speedy orgasm. It would be merely the closing of a circle, defining a part of my real relationship.

Pieter and I were still waiting for the crane in this godforsaken landscape when I headed off into the destruction, hopping tree trunks and shimmying beneath giant, fallen trees until I was sure I was out of sight of the road and any other little hovel, barn or house. I needed to find a secluded spot where I could take a shit. In the beginning, I'd found it awkward, this shitting in the midst of civilization. I judged wind direction and tried wherever possible, if not to hold it, to crap downwind. As time passed I sloughed off these concerns and acquiesced to my body; by then Erwin had come to work in the forest with us. One night as the evening dark descended, Pieter, Erwin and I shat simultaneously, a trilogy, a trinity of defecation, calling encouragement from our separate spots across another tree-strewn farmer's field.

Soil of God, I said.

Take away the sins of the world, said Erwin.

Amen, added Pieter.

We marked our piles of crap with deadfall sticks from the trees we had cut that day, branches that the local people would later collect and bundle into faggots for their woodstoves and fireplaces. I wonder now if they might have come upon our dumps as they worked and expressed their offence with shock and disgust, but I didn't think about that then. Pieter made the sign of the cross in the air — his thick workman's hand over the mound of feces.

In nomine dictum, strontium heilige aarden in Gloria, Aaamen. Shit, holy earth. Glorious father in the heavens. Aaa-men.

From my contrived wilderness privy, now, I could see Pieter surveying the destroyed forest. Behind him the nuclear chimney was like a decapitated minaret, the thin line of drifting smoke the only sign of its true purpose. Its grey concrete austerity had a monastic stillness; the forest, too, was still that morning, except for the creatures skittering about in search of safe haven. The light at that time of the year rarely opened up the sky but skimmed the clouds and bounced away back upwards. It was a diffusion — the edges of the rain-threatening clouds were a perplexing, pollution-build-up yellow. I made my way back to him over and under the felled forest.

A farmer had hobbled by. He was a small, bent, elderly man with lines etched on the lines in his face, the onset of cancer splotched along his nose and rot flourishing in his few remaining teeth. He wore blue rubber clompen; smears of fodder and dung from the morning rounds covered his overalls. When he saw me heading over, he tipped his cap, h'lo.

Hi.

He glanced out at the destruction.

Whad'ya know? he said, turning back to Pieter.

It's a job, said Pieter.

Better you than me. Stront werk, that's what it is.

The winds had raged with such a ferocity that the earth seemed to react sympathetically to our loss. At the peak of the storm, Pieter and I had huddled in bed. Seeking warmth or unity, we made love, a lick from the neck down and down to his penis. A bumblebee slammed itself repeatedly into our bedroom window, so we let it in. It nestled into a warm corner of the frame, making a confused effort to sting the glass.

Pathetic fallacy, I had said

It's not so bad, said Pieter.

Not you, I said.

We lived in an old manor house on the Prinsenhof. The tower spire on the old beer-hops factory attached to the house pierced the gathering sky. It was wrought for beauty more than function and would totter and fall as the winds reached their height. I wished the bee was Erwin slamming into the window, trying to come back. Even if he was only a bee, he could sting, make honey, let us know he was all right, alive.

I used to bring coffee up to Erwin in bed and wake him up by placing my cold hand on his sleep-warmed shoulder. He twitched me away as a horse does an insect, with a neural shiver. His eyes opened as the smell of coffee registered, and he smiled. His light blue eyes had the translucent quality of a sub-equatorial ocean. They gave off a buoyancy that is hard to describe.

Thank you, he said.

Is it good?

I sat next to him on his bed and marvelled at his beauty, at the pure awakening loveliness of him. We chatted in English, laughing at the way he put words together, more and more and more words in a hopeless attempt at meaning. I could easily have slid under the covers, my body curving into his, our skin rising excitedly to the touch; I did not.

Oh my god, I said to Pieter one night early on. He's better than you in every way.

Maybe not every way, Pieter said, sliding his hand between my legs, fingers searching through the wet. As children, Pieter and Erwin had been inseparable. Their mother had even dressed them identically, despite the fact that they were born a year apart. The familiarity of their brotherliness was reassuring to me (what returns a touch might have, now he's lost?).

Pieter and I went to bed when our eyes sunk closed at the table from reading, the wine having seeped into our dreams even, and we would huddle up close on the makeshift bed installed where an ancient toilet had once been. We were desperate to draw heat from one other in the frigid coastal humidity. We would murmur love adages in broken languages, and we would fuck. Loudly clipping each stair with his feet, Erwin would go upstairs to his room, where he occasionally had a houseguest but most nights didn't. I would think about him making the lonely trip there to his cold, empty bed. Stupidly, I was unable to fathom the way in which his loneliness was a creation of our union.

There is a photograph I took of Erwin and Pieter. They are singing together in the yellow light of a dozen candles, the wood stove open for still more light. Pieter and Erwin are leaning into one another, both wearing rust-coloured sweaters knit by old girlfriends, canvas caps — the light turning these to haloes around their heads. If I suspend my disbelief, time stopped there. They look, even on close inspection, like Siamese twins. I said this once to Erwin as we stood about in the forest one day, waiting for Pieter to fell more trees so that we could de-branch them. Erwin was smoking and swatting at me playfully with his wool scarf, wrapping the scarf around my legs and trying to trip me.

You are like Siamese twins, you and Pieter.

What's so good about the Siamese?

You know, Siamese twins are joined in body.

Ha, he said, yes. We could be joined at your hip.

I knew how to examine a branch on a felled tree and expertly remove it. Sometimes this involved slicing twice or more, sometimes from below, the chainsaw blade cutting along the curve here and then there; the tree would almost sigh as it was relieved from the tension in which that branch held it, and then it would shift into a calmer position. We cleared each forest as if we were in a ballet, dancing around each other, making short work of each tree until the field lay littered with branches and the crane or the skidder could pull our immaculate logs into an ever-growing pyramid.

Three hundred cubic metres per day. It's amazing, I said.

Each day a little more, said Erwin.

No. There must be a threshold. If you go too fast, the pattern will be disrupted and it will lack beauty.

So?

It isn't worth it, then, I said.

What's beautiful about a felled forest?

Something. Something unspeakable.

In this hurricane-hurled forest, Pieter and I trimmed branches, some huge and twisted, while we waited for the crane. There was no sense trying to cut the roots away without some mechanical help — far too dangerous. We checked the length of the tree before we sliced through the leader to make sure the trunk was free and straight. And still the cutting bands got caught regularly in the torque-prone stems. We carried wedges and a sledge-hammer around with us in order to pry the tree open if it pinched the saw's blade. The stinging nettle hid an assortment of unpredictable miseries, too, including old fencing that nicked the saw's razor edge. We had to stop every couple of trees, take out the files and sharpen our tools. Meanwhile, Pieter's skin had swollen from the nettle rash. Also, my saw kept cutting out. First it surged, then it coughed and stalled. I opened it up, cleaned the spark plug with an Opinel knife, cut out the exhaust debris. It was a day from hell, as Pieter had predicted.

As I worked, I stood on the trunk of the tree I was cleaning, shifting my weight as the tree rolled or shifted its. A wild ride and chancy. The height and unpredictability of each tree intensified my concentration. I had learned early on to jump at the slightest worrisome movement. I assessed each tree by its particularities — the way the bark turned up its spine, the direction of its fall, what lay on it and in what manner. I could climb along a tree hanging upwards of two metres in the air and work with precision and without fear. There was a thrill to it. Finally, the crane arrived on the back of a flatbed truck. The operator, a hulking giant named Paul, emerged from the cab.

'Dag, said Paul.

'Lo.

As soon as he perceived my gender, Paul began to leer at me. He smiled at me from the glassed-in booth of the crane. Whenever he spotted me and he thought I might be looking, a horny glaze came over his eyes and he put his hands down between his legs to the gearshift. He sat up high in the red crane, watching me as much as possible while he was working. Later, I would come to thank him.

Paul positioned his crane so that the jaws held the tree stem. Pieter stood as far back as he could without losing his balance and sliced through the tree as close to the roots as possible without catching dirt in the chainsaw blade. As often as not the root ball crashed back to earth right in the spot where it had emerged. The craters were filled. I noticed suddenly that Pieter had lost weight; his pants were loose on him. Thinness gave him the appearance of having grown taller. He had changed even as he regretted the possibility of moving on, changed physically. Soft down had sprouted on his chest, his manner had more room for humour, his lovemaking had become more exploratory. He was approximating Erwin's presence; we both were.

I would die without you, Pieter said to me.

No.

I would drink.

You drink now.

I moved further and further away from the racket of the

crane. What must it have sounded like, I wondered, these huge trees ripping up the earth, trees crashing into other trees, splintering with thunderous cracks. Did the small forest creatures under the roots look up, their roofs removed, their vulnerability exposed, and notice death looming with each new crash? The reactor chimney smoke swirled into a mini-twister, thrown this way and that in a smoke dance. I sat down amongst the fallen trees and ate a sandwich that I had stuck in my jacket pocket. It was a squished pair of bread slices with a thick smear of fresh butter, two speculaas cookies in between.

I could no longer see Pieter or the crane. When the buzz of Pieter's saw cut out for any length of time, I counted off the minutes it took for him to roll and smoke a cigarette. If the silence lengthened, I became alarmed, and a bilious anxiety rose in my stomach. He had become everything to me; we were inseparable. Perplexing death images dissipated only when I stood close to Pieter; when we were in bed together I felt complete. The night after the accident, Pieter and I crawled like maimed animals under the duvet. I had sorted his clothing in the upstairs laundry, held the blood-soaked cloth up to my face. I had no idea what I was doing. I had read once that Madame Curie held her husband's brains in a handkerchief for days, not able to bear the loss of his mind. I put one little bloodied wood chip into my mouth (the metallic taste of Erwin melting on my tongue), and then I shoved Pieter's sullied clothes away from me into the washing machine. I watched them agitate clean. I should have built a shrine around them, I thought later, as Pieter whimpered in bed next to me. I was not asleep; I was heartlessly alert when Pieter held me close and made love to me. It was Erwin's face and his body that came to mind.

Does it bother you that I loved him?

I am not a jealous person by nature.

I felt this comment as a heavy burden. It weighed on me. Not as guilt but as something more tangible, as if I were somehow responsible for propping it all up, holding us on the earth. Everything had an enormous heaviness. My legs moving from tree to tree were magnetized and grounded; I could not fall. The Doem laboratories had repatriated loads of vitrified nuclear waste in barrels deep in the ground; they'd dug a series of a hundred tunnels seventy-six metres beneath me, deep under the Tertiary clay that itself created a non-porous shield against any possible leakage. The little fishes bumping into the wire mesh. Erwin's hand on my throat. Even laughter carried weight. I felt the world had a boundlessness that I could not escape. And this depressed me.

Even sorrow is fleeting, Pieter said.

That's not my experience.

The crane operator was the closest when I fell. He clambered out of his machine as quickly as his giant body allowed to help me. I had screamed. Pieter was further away and took longer to arrive. Paul's hands were enormous, like grizzly paws. They lifted me as if I were a bundle of dried sticks. I had been listening to the sweet whine of Pieter's saw off to my left and back. I had looked up into the sky before giving the tree my full attention. There was a single bird grappling with the air currents. It spun midair and regained flight balance, seeming to enjoy the inevitability of its own weakness. I looked carefully along my tree, and I sliced it through. The tree became an instant catapult, grabbing me by the midsection. It hurled me in seeming slow motion in an arc some ten metres through the air before I dropped at full force into another log, spine first. I expected to die and braced myself for this inevitability. I held the spinning blade of the chainsaw as far away from my body as possible, reasoning that if I dropped the tool it might cut me in half. The space around my eyes in that instant of airborne thrust was shattered into a million quartz-like shards. In the strange expansion of time before I landed (the awful shock of pain; the catapulting tree flinging about trying to find its central calm), I sought to explore these gem-like splinters, their texture, their variegated edges, and imagine a way they might fit together to explain to me what I had become, and then wonder whether, if given the time, I could look through this clear stone of my creation to determine what had become of us.

Way Up

I felt the beginnings of a ruse only after settling myself into her matte blue 1984 Volvo 240 wagon, after the door latched awkwardly, for it was broken, and she bound it shut with a green and red mini-bungee to the back door, leaning over me as a mother does to buckle in her child, once I had nestled into the somewhat lopsided passenger seat and realized I shouldn't have come, that my instincts were all along nigglingly against coming, and if it weren't for the chance-of-a-lifetime photo opportunity to meet and shoot a childhood hero of mine (and hers and everyone else's born in the 1960s and '70s in Canada), I wouldn't have been there fondling the new lens I'd purchased for my Nikon, making small talk with this ex-girlfriend, Helen, nodding nervously as she told me that she had had abnormal squamous cells surgically removed from her cervix the week before, just ten minutes onto the highway, with no escape from here until Toronto.

The gynecologist-surgeon said it was the best damned cervix he'd ever seen, she said.

I guess he's seen a lot, I said.

Is that my consolation?

I don't know how these things work.

You used to, she said, and we laughed.

I put a cassette of the Waterboys into the player and jacked up the volume and stared out at the little strip subdivisions and dilapidated farms along Highway 16, soaked in the pale blue winter sky and basked in the heat of the northern sun as it projected false hope through the cracked windshield. Helen handed me a map drawn out on yellow foolscap; it was our route, an easy path in easy weather to the pretty little Norwegian cedar A-frame in Grafton where Jerome, Rusty and the Friendly Giant then lived. Helen had been my first love, and, as such, we were, therefore, destined to failure.

Tell me, Helen said, as she leaned in and turned down the music, How is Monique?

I thought you'd have heard by now, I said.

Oh, I'm sorry.

Don't be. It's just as well, I said. It ended before any rancour could set in.

Rancour?

I had come to believe that Monique was a rebound relationship, since its demise was generally easier to accept, seen in this light. In fact she had left me for a better-looking man with larger career prospects, etc., and to her credit she had kept him at bay long enough to make a clean break with me and a fresh start with him. She was the sort of person who didn't go in for clutter, for messy situations of any kind. I only mention this now because it was something that I liked about her and hoped to learn vicariously and eventually put to the test, once I had internalized the technique. I'd pinned a bit too much hope on Monique, I see now, and this had annoyed her sense of autonomy, no doubt. I believe she would have been good for me if she'd stuck me out long enough to let me to decongest from Helen. I don't blame her.

There was something now in Helen's tone, something overly sympathetic that made me wonder if she already knew about Monique and was using the conversational segue for some ulterior purpose. Helen was certainly not above such game playing.

Yes, bitterness, I said.

She must be clever to have figured you out so quickly, she said.

Ha, I said. Thanks.

The Friendly Giant will offer solace, I'm sure.

We spoke nostalgically then about our common favourite episode (the ice-skating one, where Jerome the giraffe wears a long scarf) and about the beautiful tension of Bob Homme's thick-fingered hand reaching down into the living room and settling the chairs, the anticipation of newness, of ever-so-slight change from day to day, and how he would proceed, making daily choices in the re-arrangement of that same mundane furniture, and how we rejoiced, our eyes turned up to the television while the quickening flute music settled us in, readied us for another blissful patch in the day when an adult, a giant even, would take us seriously.

Look up. Look way up.

Yeah.

And that boot.

Yeah, the boot.

Helen had some idea that she might like to try writing one of those exhaustive articles, in first person, in which the writer becomes obsessed with the intricacies of each eked-out detail, and, by investigating and examining the fragments that make up a life, may elicit some transformation, if not in herself, then possibly in the reader. That is, she said, where the notion of interviewing Homme had arisen. She had already done a lengthy interview with a cloistered nun who had taken a vow of silence and separateness, who was Christ's bride.

Did you ever write the article? I said.

No. I couldn't, she said. I'm more and more convinced that I don't have the mental distance needed for this kind of work. It isn't personal enough. It's all facts. Facts bore me. The papers want a slant, an angle, and I don't have one beyond the perplex-ing purity of the nun herself. God isn't really topical anymore. The media isn't interested in that kind of nuance.

The Friendly Giant isn't topical either, I said. So why are you doing this?

Helen was very carefully staring out the front windshield, or staring at the windshield, that was possible.

People choose safe places to conduct their lives, don't they? she said. You know, to act out their idealism. I was thinking I might do something esoteric on all that, you know. A far-reaching piece on people who have confined themselves to particular vocational jobs in order to maintain a certain ideology. Or I might fictionalize it, I dunno.

Has this got anything to do with the cancer? I said.

Abnormal squamous cells are a far cry from cancer, she said. And, by the way, that's a very insensitive question. She pulled a bag of chips out from under her seat, and we sat for a long while eating them, looking through the windshield as if it were a television screen, as if the road had some narrative thrust. The snow had drifted into the highway in rippled dunes, and the Volvo surfed them all the way to the 401; this motion made us laugh nervously.

I didn't mean to be rude, I said, which wasn't entirely true.

She glanced at me and said, It's pretty nasty. They sit you on this reclining chair, much like a dental chair, and they peer up into your body, having opened it with a speculum, and they take photographs through an inserted microscope attached to a 35 mm camera. (She gestured to my camera at this point, as if that had anything to do with it.)

So, you're not dying, though. Please don't go into the details, Helen.

It's still a bit unclear, she said.

And then I said, Remember that joke about the speculum?

It's not funny.

No.

Helen sped. She liked to catch the car in the wind stream of a transport truck and ride within its pull. She would tire of this, too, and would then ease closer to the immense vehicle until the hood of the Volvo came close to sliding beneath the truck's chassis, and only then would she pull out, signalling at the last minute as she overtook. She had always been an extroverted show-off, and this had appealed to me in our day, but this now was a seeming death-wish and as such was unfamiliar to me; it was a new personality trait that she had never before displayed, and I wondered where it had come from and whether there was a subtext that I was meant to uncover, whether this behaviour was in lieu of speech — a visual shorthand for some unspeakable thought — or whether it was just what it was.

I've never known you to wear a track suit, she said. Is this some new, new couture?

I knew I looked like shit. I had dressed for comfort. I had dressed as a fatalistic bachelor does, disregarding fashion sense if ever he had one. But now that I reasoned that I might die in this stretch cotton, zip-up, hooded abomination, with its wear and tear along the crotch inseam, that I might be found in this laissez-faire ensemble, dead at the hands of this maniacal pre-cancerous ex-girlfriend, discovered with her as if we still had anything to do with one another, I began to feel more considerate toward the "fashion arts," if that's not a complete oxymoron. In my defence, I'd shot a wedding the day before, compulsory suit and all, and I needed a break. I have regrets about the track suit. I really do.

We had been a couple for four years, Helen and I; we'd de-flowered each other in a field of thistle and standing hay in her parents' back fifty and shortly after set about finding ways to amuse ourselves, the stakes rising higher and higher the more bored we became with each other and our rural landscape. Helen knew that I'd "slept around on her." I did not tell her at the time, of course, even when she accused me of this once or twice in the thick of one of the arguments we endured, but I did come clean over the phone several months after we'd split up. I hadn't meant the transgressions personally, I told her. She thanked me, and I felt cleaner for the telling.

Slow down, would you?

It's too fast?

You're not being careful.

I am not careful, she said, and looked wistfully out the window at the rear-view mirror into which a red Mazda Miata appeared to be hurtling. She quickly edged out in front of the red blur, which jarred the Volvo, a car which at the best of times will comply only sluggishly and then follow through as an inertial afterthought; we wobbled about, the Miata practically buckled to our bumper. Helen glanced over at me when she thought I wasn't looking to see my reaction, and gauge my discomfort. There was a scheme under way even then; perhaps the entire conflation of events, beginning with the invitation to document the interview and ending in an attempt at my undoing, had been orchestrated. I have given up trying to see it from her point of view. I should have been more attentive to the signals, however cryptic and illusive they were. I often suffer from inattention, a tragic flaw, I suppose.

In fact, it was not until we stopped midway to Toronto at a mega-roadside gas and eats affair that her plan began to sink in, that I became aware of the trouble I might be in if, as was the case in the past, Helen intended to draw her cruel personal experiment out to its obvious conclusion. I ordered an eclair. I do not particularly like eclairs; I do not like the thick, sickly sweet custard and sugary whipped cream, nor do I like the form the delicacy takes, so reminiscent of the hot dog (and its obvious cognate); I especially dislike the tendency of the confection to spurt into a horrendous mess as I bite into it. Ordering it was a kind of extrapolation of the sort of infantile in-joke Helen and I used to have in the old days of our relationship. God only knows why I was so easily drawn into this ridiculous projection. I should never have gone there, I realize, now, in retrospect.

Get a cruller, she said.

Crueller than you, I said.

Fritter then, she said.

Apple or away?

We hadn't grown up; we'd stayed in the arrested development that our relationship had demanded in order to sustain itself, even though we hadn't slept together or really talked much on the telephone in about a year, well, a year and six weeks and two days, come tomorrow. Or maybe we just revisited this place out of comfort, fun and games. The pain of our very last night together was still skin-searing, and although the exact details of the way the end panned out were fogged by the protective capacities of whatever side of the brain takes care of that, the undercurrent of hurt, of purposeful emotional injury was still apparent from the way in which we turned our heads away from one another and spoke crisply, assuredly, into the implacable car windows and the mock-marble donut shop floor.

We were no longer in love; we were in hate and enjoying the cool confidence it was giving us. The polar opposites of detestation and adoration require the same heightened level of passion, and within the context of our little worn-out games, these are simply eroticized forms of one another. Helen triggered something primordial in me; I assure you she meant it in as mean-spirited a way as possible. She regressed me. I ordered the damned eclair in spite of her, but I see now how I played right into her hands by pointing out the largest, creamiest specimen under the glass and smiling up at the waitress, whose hair was streaked with a misstep of orange-yellow dye against her otherwise unnatural blonde and stringy do. My falsely wanton smile put the girl at such dis-ease that she almost dropped the chocolate-iced gateau and only caught it (upside down and slightly smeared) before it hit the ground.

I'll get you another one, she said.

No, I said, as I winked at the poor girl, I like it upside down.

Helen said, With a fox, In a box, In a house, With a mouse, I like it, like it . . .

Upside down or not, I said demurely, it's the biggest. I'll take it.

And then I sat down and ate it, staring guilelessly at the waitress as I fumbled with the dessert, licking custard along my index finger, the cream slipping away from the split bun and down my fingers onto the Styrofoam plate provided no doubt for that purpose. I heard Helen expounding on the history of the eclair — a throwback to ancient Roman fertility breads, apparently, baked as offerings to Venus, the eclair having an obvious penile significance, the pulsing ooze of its cream etc. etc.

Bakers had in-house prostitutes, Helen said, and men could hire them to perform certain ritualistic offerings. It was a time of great verve.

Mmm, I said. Interesting.

This *is* fun, she said. Isn't it?

I laughed loudly. I was having fun; I was having a terrific time. Any personal boundary I had cultivated in the last year had all but dissolved. I felt open and free in a way that I hadn't experienced in a great long time. This should have startled me, but it did not; it lulled me. Helen had ordered a double cappuccino and was stirring the froth slowly into the liquid. She cupped the mug over its opening and warmed her hand as she brought the beverage to her lips. Her haircut was severe in the style of her favourite 1920s writer, cut across the forehead and chopped shoulder-length in a no-fuss pageboy, most likely self-inflicted. Her cheekbones were high and her eyes tiny, giving her a slightly Asiatic look, although the pasty paleness of her complexion betrayed her Nordic heritage; she was a gorgeous mongrel, an ugly thing of great beauty, a person, whether I admitted it then or not, who held an enormous amount of sway over me, because of what she knew and remembered and stored for later use against me. Helen had an arsenal of information on me, and I had an inkling after her next sentence that she was prepared, had prepared herself, finally, and for some unfathomable reason, to use it. What a fool I was.

Remember the bus shelter games? she said.

Ah, I said, the bus games.

The bus shelter games were a series of spontaneous theatrical events devised by Helen and me to pass the time while waiting for public transport on frigid, dull Ottawa evenings. We began with witty, impromptu, real-life arguments concerning topics of intense interest to the common OTC passenger, often such hot subjects as "our abortion" or "her active gonorrhea," mostly made up, of course (none of your business which). We began these as hushed discussions, but inevitably they rose in pitch and melodrama, inviting, as they did by their very topicality, audience participation. Helen and I regularly and publicly split up in front of any number of strangers and received numerous ovations when we reunited minutes later. We suffered the pain of our subtextual hurts within these dramas, even if the arguments themselves were all lies. We cut each other up gleefully.

I should have packed up my stuff then; if I'd been mentally organized, even slightly, I would have brought my stuff into the donut shop and made my escape from there, but I hadn't, and the amount of energy it would have taken to extricate myself from this scenario felt impossibly immense. My knapsack was in the back of her station wagon, my camera gear was stowed behind the passenger seat. I had trapped myself; for years this had been coming down the pipe, and I was resigned to it in a way that surprised me; it was a kind of lucid dream. I felt I was spinning down a tube, unsure of where and how I would be spat out. And I stayed. I stayed.

She said, The resentment has been building. I've often thought it might be nice to kill you.

I'll admit I was a fucker, I said, if you'll stop this.

It hurt, you know.

I'm sorry, I said. I didn't mean to hurt you.

No, she said. Not that. The operation. It hurt.

I'm sorry about that, too. Now, stop, Helen.

This is moving too fast for me to stop it, she said, and then she said, Well, you were a real bastard, and now I've got all my memories to keep me company, and then she stood up, purposefully knocking her mug off the little Arborite table at which we sat and ignoring it as it shattered, with the remains of her cappuccino spilling, too, on the floor. Her haughty demeanour grabbed the attention of several now-slightly-less-bored customers, and that was a good enough audience for her. She pointed at me and in a voice of controlled fury drew me fully in that moment into her concept.

You philandering bastard, she said. I give you the best years of my life, my youth, for godsakes, and you thank me with a leer at any passing, any passing, uh, floozy. Enough. I've had enough of you. Keep your donut slut and the hole. And all the rest.

I apologized for all that, I said. I'm sorry, honey.

She swung around and glared melodramatically at the hapless waitress, then stomped away and out of the building, kicking the shards of ceramic mug as a final gesture of surrender to her anger.

An older couple over their muffins furrowed their brows at me, indicating fiercely with whom they sided in this live soap opera. I could only stare disconsolately into my Styrofoam plate, even as I nudged it to a corner of the table. A boy with an eruption of pink-tipped pimples on his cheeks hoed the mess out from under my feet with a jerry-built bee-mop, muttering, Excuse me, sir, could you lift? and then, Sorry, when I glanced up at him, the pathetic look of a betrayed hound my method template. The waitress was nowhere to be seen. As I slouched over to the exit, a man in a worn tweed suit and a baseball cap gave me an engaging look.

Don't let her go, he said. Run after her. I've been there, trust me.

Thank you, sir, I appreciate that advice, I said.

I knew that Helen had succeeded and I had failed, but even then I did not know the full extent or even the nature of her victory. My heart was palpitating from the adrenal rush of our real-life theatre. I had forgotten the pulsing, retributive power of public recognition, even if my performance was a poor one. I felt huge, larger than life, as I lumbered back to Helen. She was sitting in the car with her feet up on the dash, laughing. I felt like crying, my nerves were that frayed.

You should have seen them back there, I said. They loved us.

Helen chose her moment and leaned over to catch my mouth with hers, and as if it was the most natural thing in the world, we began to kiss in a way we hadn't for years, even within the relationship, her tongue and mine grasping at one another in a desperate exchange of fluid. She broke suction first, but not before my neural synapses had connected all the way down. My penis had uncurled within the (now-in-hindsight) maddeningly comfortable cloth of my jogging pants and had sprung up, forming a Barnum tent between my legs. I pulled her in toward me before her eyes could slide down to the spectacle nature was making of me.

We still have such a hold on each other, she moaned.

When she re-engaged the motor and pulled out of the parking

lot, I fumbled with the glove compartment, ostensibly in order to put the map away, and a small vial rolled out onto the compartment door. It was a nib of flesh suspended in some transparent viscosity.

That's nothing, Helen said, and reached for it.

I didn't ask, yet. I held it up and away from her.

It's . . . , I just keep it.

The tiny morsel buffeted as I shook the vial; the edges of the mass had dissipated into the solution. It was alarmingly, inhumanly pink — an almost floral pink of unnatural clarity.

Is that the solution or is that the real colour?

Just fuck off, she said.

Now I've seen everything, I'm prepared to die, I said.

A true coincidence, she muttered.

Pardon me?

Nothing.

We have argued about this since, because to my mind this last comment is the very crux of everything. I admit I didn't clearly hear her say that my wanting to die was a coincidence, but that is what I thought I heard, and so I proceed with my thesis based on this educated conjecture. Helen maintains that she said no such thing. She conveniently can't remember what she said and now has taken to the claim that she said nothing and that I've fabricated the entire exchange. If only we'd recorded our own now-more-important intercourse as well as the interview, I'd have proof of her diabolism. Helen plays the victim so very well.

The countryside had become more and more undulating, the forests larger, with patches of locust trees that would have grown only to thorny shrubs around Ottawa. Here they towered over the conifers and bent into one another as in a dance, tableauxed. The pink Canadian shield heaved out of the earth in jagged ruins where it had been blasted to make way for this arterial road. The car rushed past power poles, the bowed lines of which I focused on, rising and sinking as even my breath did in a meditation designed to distract me from the ever-less-cautious banking, passing and slip-streaming that Helen practised. The weather was changing; cumulus clouds were gathering moisture with an uncanny rapidity, and the sky had already begun a slow roil in anticipation of a storm. I was joyous when the Volvo pulled into the winding lane and parked alongside the house, and I could see the country, the dramatic skyline widening out before me; Bob Homme's property was an extensive circular mound of immense beauty. Cardinal and blue jay couples flitted from feeder to shrub. Even the crows did not seem menacing here.

I had expected him in breeches and knee-high leather boots, a medieval cowl; I had expected him to tower over me in black and white pixillation and lull me to calm. He was short, though, his towhead now grey. I could barely recognize the icon I had created in my imagination. The landscape was utterly snowbound, white crystal refraction shimmering between the scudding cloud shadows. Bob Homme did tower over me, he did, and with some inexplicable power.

How much property do you have?

Oh, lots, down to the black locust stand there and over, well, you can't see the line. It's a big rectangle of land. And you are?

The Friendly Giant took us around his property until the snow got too deep and we were forced to turn back. I didn't pay a great deal of attention to the conversation. The tone was complacent in the same way the show had been; I was calmed in his presence. I contrived any number of photographic angles, including one Homme must have been familiar with. I lay on the cold snow below him and snapped him upwards. He took us back to his home and fed us a meal his wife had cooked. Afterwards he played all his recorders for us and showed us the maquette of the living room, its miniature chairs and where they had been reglued. He brought out Rusty and Jerome and the minstrel cats. Helen slid Jerome onto her arm. It was late in the afternoon when we pulled out and navigated our way back up to the highway. The sky was now a low mass of turbidity. Already snow was slapping at the windshield. I did not notice that Helen did not wear her seatbelt. It was an oversight.

That was amazing, I said.

He didn't seem bitter to you?

Not really. No more than anyone else.

We were outside Newcastle when the snow turned to freezing rain. The wipers on the Volvo were in bad condition; they plowed over the rain as it stuck in little frozen bubbles to the windshield. The heater could not keep up with the building glacial mass either. A sane person would have slowed the car to a crawl, even pulled off the road. Helen slowed only minimally and acted as if her raison d'être was to get ahead of every transport truck on the road. She was driving about fifty but it felt much faster. Night began to fall; visibility was patchy. On an overpass near Bowmanville, the Volvo began to slide out of control; I looked over at Helen even while I was paralyzed with fear, and I saw the glint of joy on her face, the faint curl of a smile on her lips.

The car began a weary spiral; I did not count the loops we made. Cars and trucks were whooshing past us; we spun between them as their drivers leaned heavily, warningly on their horns. The Volvo began then to fly off the overpass and was only just caught by a steel guardrail, put there as our only salvation before buoyancy and death. Helen flew partially into the windshield, which shattered in response to this impact, but I was luckier; my seatbelt held me fast, and I escaped with a sore neck and a band-like bruise running on the bias across my torso.

Helen, I screamed, Helen, my God.

We are dead now, she said. You see how I loved you?

We were not dead, of course. Helen was severely damaged and slipped in and out of a coma for many weeks before she recovered her senses enough to be given an automatic wheelchair and a special temporary windshield pass that allowed her to park closer to the supermarket than anyone else. With physio, the expectation is for a full but slow recovery.

I visit her regularly, bring her books and videos that I suppose might ease the burden of her physical imprisonment. I doubt they do. I do not think she got what she wanted. Not really. From time to time I look at the photograph I took of her, but I can't remember the exact moment I snapped it, whether it was as she thrust her arm into the body of Jerome the giraffe or whether it was as she was removing herself. It isn't important per se, but I find it unsettling that my photograph doesn't act as more than just a cheap memento. I had thought the power of photography was greater, that it documented certain incontrovertible truths and could act as historical proof etc. In fact, it is as unreliable as the memory. It rests on the same precepts of what an image is, which is to say, it rests on the falsehood of every image. It is just another thing, make of it what you will. Helen's greatest achievement was to make me see that my actions have effect. Her ruse worked in that regard. I wheel her about on nice days, in between the photo shoots of wedding parties that keep me in groceries, and in my small way I try to be kind to her. We speak of trifling matters, we look up, way up, and we wonder at life's little turns.

The Vastness of the Lie

Jane Rae and Joanie were sisters, extremely close, how sisters can be. They could have been twins, they looked so much alike, but once you knew them they were acres different. Hysterical, real gasses, both of them, which is what it took to be part of the gang. We horsed around, played. Big fun was Blind Sports. Blind tag. Blind Frisbee. Blind badminton. We would close our eyes and just stand there in the ready pose or swing maniacally at the birdie. Sometimes Jane Rae and Joanie's psycho basset hound Bozer would corner the birdie on the grass and take a hissy fit. We dropped to our hands and knees and barked at the birdie, too. This convinced Bozer of his prowess as a hunter, sent him into a demented howl. The dog lunged at the birdie, snapping his fangs, then backed away whimpering, only to lunge again. And again. Teenagers ruin dogs, it's a well-known fact.

My family was invited to their family's for a BBQ. It was the first time. I was eleven. Their mum smoked so much she had yellow fingers and rotten teeth. She laughed all the time, Scotch on the rocks clinking to the beat. Mum said she was a hoot, but I didn't get the jokes — all sex and swears. Me and Jane Rae and Joanie ate hotdogs and ran around in the fields.

Horses don't eat milkweed, Jane Rae said. That's why the field is chewed down to the bare earth except for the milkweed plants. Poison. The only thing'll eat milkweed is monarchs. They're poison, too.

We opened the pods and flung the seeds around. It was great. We found sticks and went back to shove silky marshmallows on the ends and roast them black in the bonfire, peel off the char and eat the sticky goo. Night fell and fireflies came out. Jane Rae and Joanie ran inside to get empty mayonnaise jars. We caught as many of the bugs as we could and brought them inside to Jane Rae's bedroom. The lights were out, and I didn't yet know my way about the house. They'd opened the jars and let the fireflies free. I was sitting on Jane Rae's bed beside her, the hair on our arms touching. I'd never been let up past dark in the summer. There were sparks everywhere. I'd never seen fireflies before.

We wouldn't have been allowed to brings bugs inside (nothing against them per se, just that they happen to belong out of doors). It was a Rule. Frankly, my mother didn't like insects. She'd scream bloody murder and flap her arms about if a bumblebee even came near her when she mowed the lawn. I loved them. Ants were tremendous. Butterflies and caterpillars were, too. Certain yellow butterflies held funerals; I had witnessed several, so I knew. Also, ants could cart butterflies. They ate the flesh but not the wings. Bumblebees stung only if you bothered them. They didn't like Mum to mow the lawn. It disturbed them. It stood to reason that people had a lot to learn from the insect world.

I could hear Mum calling for me. It's time to go home.

I never wanted to leave. I was just wondering how Jane Rae and Joanie would catch the fireflies again when someone flicked the lights on, and there they were, transfixed by the light to the white walls. They were horrible, brown and nasty looking. Jane Rae and Joanie's dad was standing in the doorway of Jane Rae's bedroom. He was wearing a beige shirt and a loosened yellow necktie with dots, brown trousers. He was short, his hair was thinning and red. He looked a little like Van Gogh around the eyes, not the man Van Gogh but the self-portrait, all orange and fucked. We had a poster of it. My mother was crazy for him. Jane Rae plucked a firefly off the wall and popped it into her mouth, pretended to chew it.

Their dad said, It's time for you to go home and time for my girls to hit the sack.

His hand was propped on the door jamb. The blood must have been circulating away from it because the skin was pale like it never saw the light of day, and a vein running the length of it had swelled. He didn't even notice Jane Rae eating the firefly. What a gas. When he left, she shut the light and opened her mouth. The firefly flashed in her mouth and I could see it all — her teeth, her larynx, the pinkness of the flesh inside her mouth. Jane Rae was everything I wanted to become.

I didn't get to see much of them, though. They went to the public school and the United Church. My sisters and I went to the separate school, were Roman Catholic. Catholics didn't mix. In winter, the snow blowers created a long, mountainous ridge between the schools. We had gruesome snowball fights when the duty teachers weren't paying attention. Some of the older boys packed gravel into the snowballs to cut people. Separate school kids detested public school kids, since they were Godless Heathens, and it was well worth the glory and the strap if you got caught. Mike O'Connell got caught. Pierre Lapierre got caught. Kevin Kenny, who was fat and poor and who had real cooties but was nice just the same, got caught. He hadn't done anything, but he was with the others; association was a strappable offence in my school. First they tried to make you cry, and if you wouldn't cry, they strapped you until you did. They wanted visible repentance. I got caught once teasing the Tulpen twins and made damn sure to cry first off, before the leather came out. The principal thought he was Christ reincarnate. Actually he was a first-class turd.

Mrs. Tulpen called up my mum to tattle.

Your girl is beating up on my boys, she said.

Pardon me? my mum ventured. My mum despised tattle-tales worse than bugs.

Your daughter has been beating my boys up in the school yard.

Mrs. Tulpen, my daughter weighs exactly seventy-eight pounds.

I fail to see how difficult it would be for two strapping Dutch boys to hold their own.

Tell her to leave my boys alone.

The Tulpens had viral germs that you could contract by merely and accidentally brushing up against one of them. Cooties. Unless pressured by a teacher, no one went down the slide after a Tulpen. If forced into contact with one, you could pass on the germs to someone whose fingers weren't crossed. If you had contracted the cooties and had been unable to pass them on, you could expect to play alone at recess.

In order to persuade my father that I ought not to be going to church, I refused to take Communion, refused to go to confession, refused to participate in the Mass. I failed to convince him. I spent Mass observing the congregation instead of the liturgy. The Whitings, who were a family of pasty-faced asthmatics from England, sat up front. Usually one of them read aloud some illuminating Psalm, which made me puke. The Tulpen clan rose and knelt, shocking the air with cattle smells. Mr. Leie, the accordion teacher, jingled change around in his pockets. It was well known among the children that Mr. Leie was a pervert. My sister took accordion lessons from him; Jane Rae took piano. He made the girls take their shirts off and wrestle after lessons while he watched, jingling around in his pockets. Pocket pool. Kevin Kenny's dad sat three-quarters back, probing his brain by way of his nostril with an enormous index finger. By Communion he was asleep with his head collapsed into his Sunday coat. Mrs. Kenny looked straight ahead, which was proper protocol in church. You were supposed to be in union with the Holy Trinity and therefore unaware of the banalities around you. Kevin Kenny looked down, mortified that I was watching. The Catholic Church sucked. I wished to God I went to the United Church with Jane Rae and Joanie.

Thank Christ himself I wasn't Dutch. The community was rife with Dutch farmers and their offspring. They smelled of cattle and pig shit. They had enormous families which took up entire pews at church. The Dutch valued the Roman Catholic Church so much they scraped together the money to send their offspring to Catholic high school. And thank Christ I was fourth-generation Canadian-Irish and not first. My father's inherited Catholic gene had managed to wear off enough to let the Irish cheapskate gene flourish. Public school was free and so was I. At fourteen I got to take the same school bus as Jane Rae and Joanie. Life took on an unprecedented buoyancy.

Joanie. She was a self-proclaimed klutz. We would trip her for laughs, and the greatest was that she'd laugh, too. She looked a bit horsy, like her mum, but she was skinny and delicate. We made pimple jokes. She always got one doozy a month to coincide with her menstrual period.

That's quite a zit, Joanie. Quite a zit, indeed.

Heeheehee.

She always had cuts and bruises. Her clumsiness was a point of severe ridicule. We'd leer over the green vinyl bus seats, which were trimmed with white plastic piping and which smelled richly of gymnasium, and accuse her.

Joanie? Joooanie? J'accuse. J'accuse. Tell us the truth, eh? We know it anyways. Eh, Joooanie? It's old Vincent Van Gogh. Your Daddy beat you, didn't he?

Don't be silly, she'd reply with movie-star haughtiness, I merely fell down the stairs. Again.

Jane Rae and I smoked cigars with tiny pieces of hash tucked in the end. We'd meet halfway down the concession, four miles of gravel road, to smoke pin joints. We burnt our tits suntanning on their garage roof, listening to Pete Townshend, Pink Floyd, the Clash, the Police. In agony, our tits turned a mottled brown and peeled. It didn't matter. If you wanted a good tan, you had to burn first, a good base. Later, we dropped acid. Little blotter squares with Mickey Mouse and Tweetie Bird stamped on them. We knew everything. You could find out anything you wanted from books in the library. LSD was not a drug that forced dependency; we made sure first. We did not want to be addicts. We knew everything. Mushrooms were safe hallucinogens. We ate mushrooms and walked around Ottawa until we came down. Jane Rae literally peed her pants laughing, so I had to buy her cotton track pants from the Zellers. She changed into them under the bridge near the canal locks, where we left her wet jeans behind.

Do you know what?

What is it, Jane Rae?

I despise my father.

Yeah? Get to the point.

Prick. I mean it. I really hate him.

Ever do wall tokes?

Show me.

We did wall tokes, sliding up the arch of the stone bridge.

I, myself, have nothing but reverence for my dad.

Good old Peter.

You said it.

I'll never marry.

Neither of us.

Deal?

Deal. We sealed it with a high five.

Jane Rae and I would beat Joanie up, pretend. We'd pummel her within an inch. Faux punches. It was bullshit. For laughs. Larfs. The second we raised our fists, Joanie would crumble. She laughed a halting, terrorized sort of laugh that told us she knew it was a joke but that, nevertheless, the tide of the joke could sway easily out of her control. It got so that we could turn on her, point a finger menacingly and say, Watch it! and she'd drop and ball up. She looked like a curled-up fawn, a detail that fascinated us.

I got to sleep over only once that January. Jane Rae, Joanie and I went for a walk so we could smoke up, farking freezing. We ate toothpaste to hide the smell and then went back inside to watch TV shows. Their TV room was stuccoed with thick plaster and reminded me of pictures I'd seen of the catacombs where the Christians hid. We shrouded ourselves with blankets against the cold, and against the munchies, we ate salt and vinegar potato chips until our gums felt as if they were separating from our teeth. We watched *Second City TV* and leaned into one another, laughing at Andrea Martin, Catherine O'Hara, Eugene Levy and John Candy. They were brilliant. Jane Rae and Joanie's mum kept popping her head in and smiling at us. She brought us Cokes. Hers had rum in it. We told her we were planning to stay up for *Monty Python's Flying Circus* at twelve-thirty.

Oh, all right. I can tell when I'm not wanted, she said and went to bed.

Jane Rae and Joanie's dad went to bed, too. He didn't say anything but just stood in the arch of the door for a long time, swaying like a diseased tree in a storm, ready to break down. Then he disappeared. Joanie fell asleep curled up on the carpet; a grey cat slept on her hip. After *Monty Python* came a late night blue movie. When the man and the woman kissed, the camera got close, cutting off their faces until only their tongues could be seen darting into each other's mouths. Gross. They did it under shiny sheets. I'd never seen a man's thing. I only had sisters.

Secret? Jane Rae asked.

Sure.

They have purple veins in them, she confided. I saw my dad's once.

Oh, gro-oss, I said.

I was thinking, why did she have to see her father's, for Christ's sake, when, I suppose the intricacy of that thought showed up on my face. I glanced over at her and I saw everything, the truth, what have you, and I saw a sob catch in her throat and give way to a great silence, the enormity of which left room for boundless speculation.

I heard the story from my mother much later. Jane Rae and Joanie were wakened by their mum in the middle of the clearest, coldest moonlit winter's night, frost crackling in the cedar brush. Their mum whispered, Get up, get up, with the warm smell of Scotch on her breath. They drove for three days, slept fitfully, excitedly, freely, in cheap U-Nap Motels, spoon-style on sagging queen-sized mattresses on puke-coloured, puke-stained wall-to-wall pile, in an often wished-for but never before dared escape from old Vincent Van Gogh. I never saw my Jane Rae and my Joanie again, but I think of them still when I walk through a field and pick up a ripe milkweed, tear open the pod and watch the seeded lint rise and whirl into the wind, dispersing.

The Burial

Spent lilac and flowering wild rose along the sand road meant an abandoned farm. Primary and secondary growth — willow, alder, birch, white and red pine — arched up here and swallowed the space where the log house had tumbled, burned down or been dismantled and relocated. A woman had planted the shrubs, and the roots took hold with a tenacity that the settlers themselves could not always match. They moved on, they died horrible deaths, they simply worked themselves into early graves and were planted six feet under, too deep to bloom. Duncan Wilkie's land had seen neither lilac nor rose. It had seen poverty, whisky, blind raging aggression, sexual misconduct, three Jersey cows, a flock of pecked laying hens, a motherless child going by the name of Darlene, a worm-infested apple orchard, and, seasonally, row on row of potato bugs doing their best to consume the entire crop. The mother died in childbirth long before she had time to stoop, dig a hole and plunge any sort of spring flowering hope into that farm.

Jennifer McBride, who was driving along the concession road, twisting lid after lid from airport wine samplers, emptying them down her gullet and then flinging the bottles out the open passenger window, had not the foggiest clue about all that history. Neither did she give the slightest iota of a fuck. She was out for a joyride in her ancient yellow Volkswagen Golf, itself held together with silver duct tape, epoxy and need. The weather was hot and dry. The sky was piercingly blue, so clear that it appeared as if each tree, each old building, even the clouds cut their shape out from it.

Jennifer was drunk, naturally. She turned to her non-existent passenger and said, Excuse me. And she flicked an empty miniature Beaujolais bottle across the passenger seat and out the window. It nicked the mirror, shattering both mirror and bottle; light glinted off the shards, giving a stop-action effect.

You needn't be so self-righteous, Jennifer muttered. No one drives here anyway.

There was no response, of course. Had there been a passenger, it might have been Maude McBride, Jennifer's once legal guardian, proven guardian angel and consummate auntie. She wasn't there, not because she was laid up with a sprained ankle, which she was, but because she would have spoiled Jennifer's fun. Her voice was there, always there, inside Jennifer's head, telling her exactly what to and what not to do. Jennifer ignored all of that better judgment. At the huge weather-worn No Trespassing / Défense d'entrer sign on the threshold of Duncan Wilkie's property, she made a left turn and lurched with the car into the overgrown lane, bouncing over a broken culvert into a shallow ditch. The car stalled. Jennifer felt suddenly tired and laid her mousy, permed head on the steering wheel, turned the radio off and fell asleep. An hour passed before she shook herself awake.

The nap had given her a headache. Jennifer crawled over the gearshift to let herself out the passenger side — the driver's side door had long been jammed closed — and after walking up a small incline discovered that she was on an abandoned farm. A pair of sugar maples danced together behind a log house. The chest-high grass was rife with weeds: loosestrife, goldenrod, vervain, daisy, all swaying southward in a soft breeze. Around the field grew a dense and mature forest of pine, spruce and hardwood. Just south of the log house, the ghost of Duncan Wilkie stood sentinel, wondering what fortuity had brought him and his land, after so long a century, this pretty girl. It troubled him that she looked through him as if he weren't there.

Jennifer surveyed the slightly rolling topography, the rocky knoll near the forest, the cumulus clouds which had formed above the tree line, and in spite of the fact that she was half corked, or perhaps because of it, the view captured the small fraction of her heart that hadn't been scratched beyond recognition in her twenty-six short years.

Oh my God, this is beautiful, she whispered. She knew immediately that she wanted to be there, wished there was a mathematical formula to measure the quality of beauty.

The property had hardly been used in thirty years. Yves Delorme had a few head grazing there, but after a couple of his best milkers were stolen, he shackled the rest together like a chain gang and shuffled them back to his barns in Curran. With a farmer's sensibility, he had cut a great hole in back of the log house for his tractor, but keeping the Ford on the property had proved a misery, too. Bats shit on it and vandals took it for joyrides in the field until it ran out of gas. Yves refilled the tank, another ten dollars later, and brought the tractor home too. Except for the firewood he and his sons hauled off it every fall, the property had been a dog. He had bought the land from Duncan Wilkie's granddaughter as a favour, five thousand dollars he could ill afford. She'd taken the money and moved to Vancouver, where at least there was work. She had wanted out; the whole thing oppressed her. And now, but for a short line of headstones in the cemetery at the end of Concession Seven, there wasn't a Wilkie left in the region. Jennifer found Yves eventually, inquiring after his whereabouts at the post office.

Down the road, the white and yellow house there on the right, you can't miss it.

Yves was peering over the hay bales stacked in the loft. He smiled at her and said, You speak French?

Un petit peu, je m'excuse, je suis Anglaise.

That's nothing. We are all crippled, eh? He showed her his right hand, not much left there, a couple of fingers. The thumb, the pinkie and the one beside it he'd lost to a cutditioner five years earlier. Yves's second son, Martin, searched high and low for over an hour, while his first son, François, drove him to the clinic in Plantagenet. Bad luck. Scouring the drying hay only uncovered writhing nests of newborn field mice, transparently naked, blind, too red to be human. No sign of his father's three lost digits until the middle of winter, when the best milker found one in an opened bale and flung it. A red-winged blackbird caught it midair and pecked the half-rotted flesh from the bone. François found the knuckle, still articulating, and the nail, caked (as always) with soil, under the cast-iron water trough and identified it as his father's thumb. Yves strung it on a plumber's chain and wore it around his neck, c'est pas mal comique, but Beatrice called it sacrilège, so on one of his cemetery maintenance rounds, Yves buried it in the pre-purchased family gravesite.

I want to buy the farm on Concession Seven.

Not for sale.

I could rent it then.

It's off the hydro line. There's no service there.

Can I meet your wife?

Yves climbed down from the loft, slapped the dust, seeds and flowers from his clothes and brought her to the house. It was clapboard, painted yellow, with a rickety veranda undulating on three sides. Pansies grew in rows in front, and a claw foot bathtub half-buried vertically in the grass, painted powder blue on the outside, blindingly white on the inside, sheltered a varnished concrete Madonna, arms outstretched, heart dripping red latex blood. Lilac, peony, bleeding heart had long since flowered. It was July.

Jennifer stood, each foot planted on its own linoleum tile, and practically begged.

I'll pay you to help rebuild the log house. I'll rejuvenate the land. Look, I have first and last in cash in my pocket. You'll end up with an improved property and income.

Beatrice stuck her finger in one pink impatiens and brushed the pollen into another.

Patience is a flower you have to tend your whole life, she said.

It was a lesson for which Jennifer was not yet prepared. She smiled in a way that left a bad impression.

Why there? asked Beatrice. It's not safe. No one will find you if something happens to you.

I'll run a phone in.

C'est cher, cher.

I have money, Jennifer responded, and when she saw that wouldn't be enough information she added, I'm a teacher. I'm on a leave of absence. I was just in England, studying mathematics. I teach high-school calculus.

Beatrice smiled. I have family in Liège, a great uncle. A priest. I was in London.

I think he is dead by now, my uncle. It must be nice to travel.

Yes, Jennifer lied, I had a fine time.

They shook her hand and waved her off. We are old, they seemed to say. Haste makes waste. We'll think about it. Talk to our children. Weigh the details. You think about it, too, peut-être, and come back when the hay is all in and the garden vegetables put by. The truth was that Beatrice didn't like the soft sell.

Elle est folle, said Beatrice before they started to eat their evening meal, before the blessing even.

Mais riche.

Yves, c'est rien qu'une swampe. Plus the house is haunted. If the mosquitoes don't get her, the ghost will.

She has money. We need money. It's a perfect affair.

She is just a child.

What harm can she do?

Halfway through the meal, Beatrice wiped her hands on her apron. Is she Catholic, do you think?

Elle est Irlandaise.

The Irish are drinkers.

Surely not the women.

Nowadays even the women.

But she is Catholic.

Oui. Ça c'est bien.

Beatrice ate with her eyes on her food while Yves glanced up between mouthfuls, yearning for his woman's pronouncement. It came as a relenting twist of mouth, a minuscule shrug of the shoulder, a nod, and Yves jumped up from the Formica-topped kitchen table, slapped it with his open palm, yelped for joy like a man newly revived, for he had always secretly hoped to become a landlord, and now, at age seventy-nine, he would achieve it. Why anyone would want to live in a swamp is beyond me. But even so, Beatrice smiled at her animated husband. Maudite merde, my hip hurts. Yves slumped back down into his chair.

Jennifer bought herself a six-pack of Chianti and took a room at the Bourgetel, its beige paint faded from a certain insidious yellow popular in the fifties, at a price of fourteen dollars a night, and for a week she tolerated the squeaking bedsprings, the grunting half-pleasures, the corpse-waking snores, the howling nightmares, the coughing vomits, and the discotheque bass of the dislocated around her, and then, calculating what little time and money she had available to dismantle and rebuild a log house, with exactly no skills whatever, she headed back out to the property. She swung the Volkswagen off the main road and drove to Lot 15, pitched her burgundy dome tent behind a camouflage of alder, parked the car behind a stand of young jack pine and went exploring. She trampled daisy, lichen, horsetail, buttercup, chicory. Her swishing approach frightened away all manner of beast and bird. It seemed as if the land was completely barren, so still was it.

She walked around the log house assessing the damage. Joists were missing, one wall was in the process of collapsing, there was no foundation. She counted the logs, measured the spans, measured the window holes, climbed up the rust-eaten oil drum that had been used in its day as a makeshift woodstove and hoisted herself onto the second floor. Shards of crockery, medicine and whisky bottles, bird nests, droppings, the coo of pigeons, the click of bats restlessly shifting. The stress of this intrusion created a nervous heat in her chest.

Lath, she said aloud, plaster. The whole thing'll need to be dismantled, each piece numbered, new logs hewn, chimneys rebuilt, flooring, paint, windows, roofing, a cellar, a foundation, plumbing, at least a hand pump, I'll need an outhouse, a bathtub. Am I crazy?

Coo. Coo. Coo. Coo.

Click, click, click.

Jennifer eased herself back down, sat in the grass outside the log house, uncorked a bottle she had picked up at the little liquor trailer in Bourget, set to calculating and listing. She had four months worth of salary left. She knew that she wouldn't be going back to work at the high school, even if they'd have her, which was doubtful since she'd been caught red-handed (red-lipped?) drinking, caught with the cork off a bottle of Saint Emilion (Grand Cru, 1979 — she had money then) and been accused of not knowing the time and the place. This was silly, of course. Time and place were the measure of motion. She'd made a life study of it. Still, they'd suspended her. So she'd have to stretch out the dollars, live low.

Her financial security was really ground down. Six months in Belgium enduring a quickly souring love affair and a secret abortion, followed by a three-week drunken sojourn in Paris. These had cost her, and not just in cash. She'd tried suicide. Sort of. She'd gone out and bought a nice, thick piece of cord with which to hang herself but had ended up wrapping her luggage with it and coming back to Ontario. Aunt Maude hadn't been that surprised to see her, her mind was addled with the early stages of Alzheimer's disease, and she was laid up with the sprain.

I've got to find a place of my own, Aunt Maude,

Yes. Yes. But have you found your mother yet?

I'm not looking for my mother. Jennifer had a Christly headache scratching away at the frontal lobe of her brain. She still stunk from the boozy flight.

Deluded as usual.

Look who's calling the kettle black.

Don't you dare snap at me. I'm ill.

It's just that you're my mother.

Don't flatter yourself.

Maude was, though. The real mum had been packed off somewhere after the delivery. The real dad was Maude's rogue brother, a hermit, a ne'er-do-well. Maude had done all the bringing up Jennifer had got or wanted. Jennifer was avoiding Maude. She didn't want to tell her about Jakob. She didn't want any false sympathy or homegrown wisdom. She didn't want the affair placed in context; she did not want words with which to describe it. It was finer and more deliciously painful to know the scene by heart, its utter loss. She didn't want that clarity sullied with Maude's half-remembered and embellished similar experience. And Jennifer could never tell her aunt about the abortion. There was no story there, only a lack of one, an unfathomable lack. And therein lay the whole story of her life — the drink in place of resolution, leaving instead of staying, the constant appeal of death in place of life. Jennifer's tendencies could be symbolized by this one event — the male nurse's fingers allowing themselves to be crushed by hers, the whining metallic pain, the sucking away of life, however small, and the unallowable sorrow. Her tendencies could easily be symbolized by this general failure to engage in life.

And if your mother had values like yours, where would you be? That's what Maude would say, Maude who did not approve of abortion. She didn't approve of affairs or alcohol drinking, either, since they led to things like abortion. The long and short of it was that Maude didn't much approve of Jennifer.

I'll be going then, said Jennifer. She unwrapped the Volks from storage as quickly as diplomacy allowed, pulled out of Maude's barn and started driving.

Yves was at the cimetière, digging a grave. Heart attack. Young father. Up and dies.

C'est pas le diable bon. It's better to die slow. Bout par bout. Piecemeal. A finger here, a hip there, the odd tooth. He gave a hearty laugh. He was unconcerned with the worms all around him. Those unfortunate enough to be severed by the shovel writhed back into the earth to regenerate.

The earth is good here, should be a garden.

He tossed the shovel up and hoisted himself out of the grave, pulled off his olive Co-op cap, wiped the sweat there away with the crook of his arm. The sun had baked a line across his forehead. The fissures inside his crow's feet were white, like a baby's skin. His hands were the colour of blackened firebrick right to the cuffs of his red plaid shirt. Farmer's tan. Yves was old enough to remember the last shanties, the dwindling forests, the ever shrinking sticks, the arrival of the drunken coureur des bois every spring, and the burials, drowned heroes, drowned fools. He could hear them singing.

> *You shantyboys, you drivers, come list while I relate*
> *Concerning a young riverman and his untimely fate,*
> *Concerning a young riverman so manly, true,*
>   *and brave —*
> *It was on the jam on Gerry's rocks that he met*
>   *his watery grave.*

He had stayed away from that damned Rideau, kept at his digging, couldn't swim to save his life. His father had come across the river more than a hundred years ago, farming potatoes for the shanties, digging graves. Yves's life was inherited. He had dug his father's grave, the first he'd dug alone, then his mother's, then an uncle drowned in the Rideau, his sister died of pneumonia, his daughter from polio. He got good practice, got good at digging.

You keep digging and the tears turn to sweat, he had once confided to Beatrice.

With a cousin, he shared the contracts to dig for five local cemeteries, three Roman, the others, like this, Anglican. Duncan Wilkie's wife, Isabelle, was the first ever buried in this one. She just kept bleeding after the baby was born. Old Wilkie drank himself into an early grave. There was his stone beside his wife's.

Yves scrubbed them with bleach once a year to keep the moss down. Darlene's headstone said she lived to fifty-three, thirty years older than her own mother when she died. Yves remembered seeing her only once. A sad sight.

Darlene must have been twelve, older than Yves then, when he and his father came to pick up the remains of Duncan Wilkie. She was standing in the doorway of the log house, hugging the jamb as if it were a giant and secure parental leg. These were the pictures Yves's mind conjured up for him when he thought of the Wilkies: the girl in the door and another of the girl standing by the oil drum woodstove. The clunk of wood on steel was the musical accompaniment, a crack of ignition and then the relieved stare. Wilkie died with his eyes open, ochre as cat piss, his skin stretched over his skull like grey tissue paper detailed with burst capillaries, red and blue. And the stench: whisky rose off him from every pore. Even in death the spirit oozed. Yves never took a drink, even medicinally, after seeing all that.

The little girl, Darling, Wilkie called her, had been preyed upon and overloved, embraced and abandoned. As she watched the strangers wrangle the corpse of him, she could think only of Wilkie's daily morning evacuation, which encapsulated so minutely, so intimately the extremes of passion she felt for him. The outhouse stood midway between the barn and the log house, on a spot where Jennifer McBride would cut sod and plant seed, eventually grow enormous carrots, wipe them clean enough with her bare hand and eat them raw. The shitter was made with tongue and groove barn boards, weathered to grey, pocked with woodpecker drill holes. The slanted roof was clad with corrugated tin salvaged from the dump. Light came in through a small heart-shaped hole in the door, disadvantageously placed so as to pierce Wilkie's eyes in the middle of a movement if he happened to forget and look up, as he sometimes did in order to achieve a full-throttle grunting push. Then he'd swear to Christ, Jesus, Mary and Joseph, and the day would be damned. Everything depended on the quality, quantity, and rhythm of Darlene's daddy's morning shit. She'd watch him stumble out to the crapper, his stunted, boxy form lunging down the incline, his red, wispy hair shooting out from under his felt hat, and she'd wait for his exit, itself not unlike a great expulsion, and the pronouncement on the day it brought with it.

What had her mother seen in him, the ruddy bastard? The derelict, cocksucker, bootlicker, ass-wipe, arsehole, sot, fuckwit, boozehound, piece of shite? The lexicon was his — irony there — but the sheer veracity of the words made her suck in breath, gave her a private power when he crawled under the feather tick, hallucinating, so drunk was he, and called her Isabelle.

How I've missed you, Isabelle. With every pulse of him she needed that vocabulary, chanted it mindlessly to obscure the rut and bring her sanely to the cuddle.

Dear Isabelle, I cherish you, I do. She never sought to break the spell, never said, It's me, Daddy, it's Darlene, Darling. She assumed, likely rightly, that if she did, it would end in a beating, in hurt, anger, broken things and utter hatred. For Daddy, she didn't mind pretending to be the mama she never knew.

When she was nine and could stay alone, he went up for the Hamiltons of Hawkesbury in the winters and left her be in order to lead the squalid life of a shantyman. It kept him dry six months of the year and gave her respite. But he came back, always made up for lost time in the spring by drinking himself blind and extracting bodily payment in one form or another from her for the various levels of poverty he endured. When he was away, she taught herself reading from a couple of catalogues, looked after the livestock. A neighbour came, weekly and of her own accord, to check in.

You okay?

Yup.

After Duncan Wilkie died, Darlene left it all behind. Neighbours took her in, she married one of them later, never mentioned Duncan again, nor Isabelle, and the farm passed silently to her own daughter when she died. But the place was said by some to be haunted, by others merely tainted. If you believe what people say . . .

Yves, driving down Concession Seven back to Curran, spotted

Jennifer's dome tent and then Jennifer, standing by the log house, so he pulled the Ford tractor into the lane and scared the living Christ out of her. She tossed her notebook quickly over the wine bottle and thought, Now they'll never let me stay. No Trespassers, the sign was clear in both official languages.

Yves hopped up off the seat, which sprang upright with a complaining, whinging see-saw of rusty springs, and walked over the dell to her with a sprightliness that, but for an almost undetectable hobble, camouflaged the crippling effect of his lumbago.

Félicitations, neighbour, he said. In his youth, Yves could charm a snake. His eyes had a sparkle that made the girls want to climb in.

You're joking.

When do we start work? He bobbed his head in the direction of her rough calculations and building plan.

You're not joking.

We gonna rebuild Wilkie's house for three weeks, then she's done. Rent is one hundred dollar a month. Take it or leave it.

Take. Take. I'll take it. Who is Wilkie?

Crazy old chantier. Long dead and buried. He don't bother you no more.

A sweeter lie was never told. Duncan Wilkie's ghost pulled off his battered felt fedora and placed it gingerly on his chest.

God rest his soul, he said, with mock sobriety. He was standing in the depression where once the outhouse stood. He would stand there waiting for three weeks as the work went on around him and act as if he wasn't there, which was easy because everyone instinctively kept clear.

Yves's two sons did most of the bush work. Jennifer hired some local thugs to come with their mini-crane to help dismantle the structure. She scrubbed each log with TSP and a bristle brush and numbered it to be puzzled back when the foundation slab was poured and dry and all the pieces cut and ready. Jennifer bought old single-paned, mullioned windows from a salvage warehouse, bought a cookstove, a parlour stove for heat, a claw foot bathtub, an iron bedstead, found a table in the dump and at the ubiquitous vente des garages a hooked rug, a rag rug, kerosene lamps, an old hand pump, shelving for her books. She dug a trench and laid pipe from the old well to the log house, had the water tested (clean as a whistle after the snakes were removed), and dug an outhouse at the sheltered side of the house, downwind, eastward. The house was back together in two weeks. The roof went up in two days. Beatrice organized a bee to chink outside and in, which went well until Duncan Wilkie's ghost realized the participants were from the church, at which point he stuck his leg out to trip all those who crossed his path.

Sons of bitches.

Jennifer was camping on the hard ground, eating in diners or out of cans heated over a fire. Nobody was at her about her drinking, and even though she had the misery of washing her clothes and herself in freezing cold water drawn by hand pump into the claw foot at the well and fending off the rodents snooping in her food stash, the night sky was hers, the stars, the fireflies, the cool, still summer air. She thought she could literally taste her new life, nestled in the cosy log house, and the flavour seemed to intensify at each completed stage until she felt she would burst from the sensation. But really all she tasted was possibility. Nature was showing its wholeness to her, and she mistook the revelation as her own. Time would tell.

As housewarming gifts, Beatrice brought red and white gingham curtains and a brass crucifix. Had Beatrice known how compelling Jennifer found the imagery of hanging, had she known that Jennifer would use the very hanging cord she had bought so purposefully in Paris as a tie-back for the curtains, she would not only have brought something more banal but also would have understood the ironic, querying look on Jennifer's face. Instead Beatrice put the look down to drunkenness, which, quite frankly, rang true. Jennifer, who had been subtly drunk throughout the construction, was now, at its finale, openly, gaily, unabashedly sauced. She cooked beans and pork, baked yeasty bread, cracked open Blue Nun and Hochtaler and made a party. Yves went home to fetch his father's violin, and everyone danced a set, passing the hat from head to head.

Beatrice whispered in Yves's ear while he played, She drinks, you see.

Mais Bea, c'est une party. But Beatrice didn't like it.

Madame Beatrice, ici, ici. Jennifer got maudlin, cornered Beatrice and confided the abortion to her. How was I to keep it after he left me? Answer me that.

You're tired, Jennifer, said Beatrice. We've overstayed our welcome.

Beatrice nodded to Yves, and within minutes the entire group was shuffling out the door, hugging goodbye, shouting thank you, thank you.

Duncan Wilkie's ghost came around the corner of the log house after the guests had departed. Jennifer was standing, dishevelled and lopsided, against the door jamb. He took her hand, bowed into it and kissed it.

I overheard your tragedy, he said. As a shantyboy I've seen it, too, sudden death. It's a miserable loss and I'm terribly sorry. I also wanted to mention that I appreciate your fixing up the house.

I'm not tired, she whispered to Beatrice's receding form, I'm empty. I feel like shit.

She turned and slumped into the house, slamming the door in Wilkie's face.

Women, he said. I'll never understand them.

Jennifer awoke in the night under an unravelling quilt Maude had made for her when she was a child. The dissipated morning light seemed to hold the dew suspended as it pressed up and through the log house windows. She sat up in bed and watched the mist settle in the field, watched the shifting dark shadows clarify in form, listened as the lows and soft exhalations emerged as disparate emanations. The realization that she was surrounded by a herd of moose rose from the pit of her stomach, grabbed the organs in her chest, her heart, her lungs. Awestruck, she ducked back into bed and hid, peeking up over the sill to witness again and again, surreptitiously, the wonder of her smallness. They were grazing with leisure and contentedness, making their way toward the forest, the beaver swamp that flooded the back corner of the property; they were headed home. She watched until the last twig of brush stopped swaying and they disappeared. A loneliness, not for company but for selfness, pervaded her again, and she treated it symptomatically and manually with her second and third fingers, a pumping motion in the soft inner skin of her vagina. This cure's efficacy would wane in time, although Duncan Wilkie's ghost hoped and prayed not. He had climbed up the wooden fire ladder and was enjoying the view.

Aye, she's ripe for it, he mumbled while rubbing away at his own crotch.

Jennifer looked up toward him and focussed on the crucifix, which had somehow found its way onto the wall beside that very window. Looking at the brass fixture, she felt an aesthetic longing. How picturesque she would have looked, twirling naked there in that Parisian hotel with the autumn shadows playing on her skin, a mere object, life simplified. Duncan Wilkie watched her face, tiny tears waiting and waiting but never able to drop away. The sight threw him back in time to a vision of his wife's frightened face, peering around the stall in the barn. The emaciated tabby cat was rubbing figure eights around his boots, hoping for a squirt from the teat he was milking. It was an early, he hoped false, labour — a vain hope. He was meant to fetch the local midwife, but as the road was a quagmire, the midwifery fell to him.

The popular notion was that no man should witness his wife birthing. He pressed into her back, tried to soothe her for most of the day. Isabelle was exhausted, broken, the mechanisms in her body began to stop. Duncan Wilkie had seen this sort of thing before. To save the child, he reached into his wife, grabbed the baby's squished and bloodied head and yanked it out, nothing to it, not unlike calving. It was a girl; the name they had chosen was Darlene. He fed her on cow's milk and neglect and she thrived. But Wilkie shrank from missing Isabelle and, burying pleasure with the wife, got on, finding emptiness in the daily routine of life and emotion in lust and hate and whisky.

I was not always detestable, thought Duncan Wilkie's ghost.

It's just destiny unwinding and therefore nothing to do with me.

Jennifer drove out to Rockland, did her groceries for the week, stopped in at the liquor store for wine and the second-hand store for more warm clothing. On the drive home she spotted a sign: Puppies for Sale.

That's what I need. It'll keep the animals at bay. Collie-shepherd-part-wolf-that's-what-they-all-say. It was cute, round bellied, all-forgiving. She named him Wolf and he became a constant companion, protector and annoyance when he tried to defend her from passing cars by attempting to throw his teeth into the rolling tires.

Christ, animal, you'll get yourself killed.

She tied him up to teach him a lesson. She beat him. These ploys failed to keep him from the chase, but they did make Jennifer marvel at the extent of her own cruelty and the pure violence to which she could succumb. She held Wolf's throat, shook him wildly and screamed at him, kicked him. He would strain, yelping at the chain, biting for his freedom, and she would give it to him, finally, out of nauseating remorse. Then, with tears building, she would apologize to the dog as if to a child, rocking him, holding him until the animal squirmed away, crouched to play, barked forgiveness.

As fall gave way to winter, she set to work on the garden, turning the sod, constructing a scarecrow out of deadfall and old clothes, a felt hat she had dug out with the grass. She planted winter wheat as a green crop. The earth was rich and would grow good vegetables. As the first sprouts urged their way from seed, Jennifer had her first misgivings about her ability to cope alone on the land. The weather changed drastically, a wind rose from the north and dumped a foot of snow on the ground. The car engine wouldn't turn over for love nor money, and she hadn't even thought to buy a snow shovel, much less arrange for a plow to come through. She had no firewood to speak of, no phone to speak into.

I'm an idiot. Jesus wept, I'm stupid.

When the first snow melted and the Volkswagen revived, she

drove to the pay phone outside the tavern in Curran and put in a call to the Bell. It cost $2,465 to run the line underground, almost running her into the ground along with it. But now she could call out at least. She organized the firewood, the plowing through Yves. She bought a shovel at the convenience store. She bought a little coat for her car battery and long underwear for herself. She borrowed a chainsaw from François and practised starting it until her hand blistered and her neck stiffened.

It didn't matter that the cold fronts were moving in, Jennifer was prepared for a glacier. Lucky. It was a season of brutal wind, unprecedented snowfall, bitter biting cold. Jennifer loaded the entrance of the log house with firewood so she wouldn't have to cut through the snow and ice that built up around the little stacks of wood outside. While this arrangement was economical, it fed her tendency toward dormancy. Jennifer pushed open the door to let Wolf out, but she herself stayed put, next to the parlour stove — too warm, still, furious at the weather, furious at herself, furious. After a heavy snow, days after sometimes, Yves would make it over to plow her out, shake his head when he saw that she hadn't bothered to shovel off the front stoop or the path to the outhouse, and he would do it for her. She always invited him in and made a pot of tea, and they would talk, unfolding bits of their lives like scraps of paper found in the bottom of pockets — grocery lists, things to do, discarded bills turning to lint, history.

He told her about the early hardships, about epidemics, the hunger, stories his mother had related about foraging for roots, mushrooms, berries, edible plants. One neighbour had died after eating the blood-red berries of a nightshade. He told her about losing his fingers, about his wife's devotion, and as they watched the last of the snow melt on the other side of the window, he told her about the time the wandering Jew was overwatered and dripped down Beatrice's favourite Virgin Mary icon.

Beatrice, she run to the priest to tell him her icon is crying. Catholics, they look everywhere for a sign. Me, I go to Mass, I go confess, I eat the Host, for me the sign is in the plants growing, that's a good enough mystery.

Jennifer smiled at him. He was kind. How do you do it? she asked.

Do what?

Dig graves.

They have to be dug. I'm a farmer so I dig anyway. Digging helps me live good. Winter is over, he said. When are you going back to teach? You're a teacher, so you got to teach.

I applied to supply teach for the township schools. I better get something, too, before my money runs out and I can't cover your rent.

It's time you turned over the garden, he said as he left. I put a shrub from Beatrice over near the garden for you.

Jennifer poured herself a glass of wine as soon as he left. And another, and another. It was late afternoon. Yves was right. Spring was edging in. The trees were in bud, the geese were returning, the moose were stripping bark off saplings, waiting for the first grass to emerge, and the worms in Jennifer's little sod garden were awake, writhing, working. But Jennifer couldn't move.

Yves took off his boots at home and set them to dry in the summer kitchen. Beatrice was dishing out stew. The bread was on the table ready for him to slice.

I was at Wilkie's place, Yves announced.

Is she drunk?

Je pense que oui.

She's dangerous to herself out there. Maybe we should evict her.

Non. She's okay. She's sad.

You don't cure sorrow with wine.

C'est vrai. But maybe you can fill an emptiness. Beatrice, I can't kick her out.

Mais, Yves . . .

I've seen it before.

Eat, Yves. It's not our business.

Jennifer kept drinking until the bottle was empty and then opened another. She drank and watched out the window, watched the scarecrow flap about in the breeze, take on a life of its own. The day wore on. From the garden, the ghost of Duncan Wilkie watched her. His skin twitched nervously with each glass raised, and it aroused him, the purple tinge on her lips. By night a southern wind picked up, bringing with it a warm front. Jennifer opened the window.

Stop staring at me, she yelled. But it didn't. She pulled on a denim jacket, a yellow tam and billy boots and went out into the wind. She was so drunk, it took her ten minutes to stumble, right herself and weave her way to the scarecrow.

How dare you stare at me, she mumbled to it and began disrobing the thing, flinging the damn hat away, ripping the old plaid shirt to shreds. She grabbed the straw head and tried to pull it off, finally bending the scarecrow in half and embracing the skull in a headlock. The straw hair was the colour of Jakob's. She had never loved anyone's hair as much as she did his. She grappled with the straw head, trying to dismember the thing and release herself from memory's hold. Duncan Wilkie, enervated, let himself be thrown about for a while, but then he fought back, bumped her over with his brawny chest, lay down atop her, pulled away her trousers — women were not meant to wear trousers, they were such a great hassle to remove. He found a breast under the shirt and started sucking on it.

What the fuck do you think you're doing? She tried pushing him away. He kept her steady with the fat part of his palm pushing down on her pelvis, his fingers holding her like a bowling ball.

Get the hell off me. Who are you, anyway? She struggled to get away.

He let go her nipple long enough to answer. I'm the ghost of Duncan Wilkie, come back to love you.

The comment had the opposite of a sobering effect. It let the full drunkenness overcome her. She floated away with it, let Duncan Wilkie's ghost caress her away into the most ethereal of orgasms. Wolf woke her up, pawing and lapping at her face, whining. Jennifer was filthy, had fallen asleep in the garden. She was still completely drunk.

God, how pathetic, Jennifer murmured as she staggered inside. She sponge-bathed at the sink and looked out at the havoc she had wrought in the garden. The scarecrow lay in pieces, strewn about, with earth caked everywhere. She watched the torn cloth flap about in the wind like a flag, and she cried a torrent of stored-up tears. Then she went out, bundled the broken body together, tossed it in her wheelbarrow with the spade and the bare-rooted shrub, and took the lot to the end of the lane. She dug a hole fit for the mutilated remains of a scarecrow and buried them under Beatrice's lilac. The lilac would send forth only one flower that first year, but eventually it would rise up as a glorious tree, fragrant with spring, and become the landmark for the McBride place, which is how Wilkie's farm came to be known.

The Mortification of Frances Brady

I did not feel well. Ross McDowell and I were necking in the dairy barn. Necking wasn't a sin or anything, they didn't ding you for it at your beatification, but it wasn't a brilliant, noble activity either, especially on a Sunday, which this was. I didn't think much of Ross McDowell as a kisser. He was all teeth and spittle.

This is bordering on revolting, I said.

Ross said, Beggars can't be choosers.

His comment perplexed me. I had neither begged nor chosen. He rubbed up against me like I'd seen cattle do at fence posts to get at an itch. Agnes and Patsy, my sisters, were eavesdropping two stalls over, making obnoxious sucking noises — wet kissing their own palms and giggling convulsively. Patsy was the baby; I could forgive her. Agnes was stupid; I could never forgive that. But the fact was, I was the eldest and expected by my parents to mind them. I was stuck with them. Ross McDowell plunged his tongue behind my teeth, something he'd been working at for some time. My virginity, I knew, had more or less been shattered.

I really was not well. The first rumblings of intestinal disaster had come in church after the sacrament of Holy Communion. I knelt, looked up to the plaster Virgin, traced my finger along the lacquered maple pew, along the bubblegum-inlaid inscription ("piss") and felt my bowel cramp. I had a terrible time swallowing it, the body of Christ incarnate, but finally the little wafer of holy cardboard disintegrated and washed down. Ross McDowell clutched my bottom and pressed me closer. A little bubble of gas found its destined route. The cramp slid downward. I farted.

Excuse me, I said, breaking suction.

Oh, God Almighty. You really cut them thick, Frannie.

Agnes and Patsy were jubilant. They reared their ugly heads over a lowing Holstein and mooed. I longed for a quick death.

SBD, said Patsy.

Silent But Deadly, said Agnes.

You've let a fluffy, said Patsy. A feather fart. An angel fart.

It was the cow, I said.

It was the cow, they mocked. Moo.

It was the Holy Ghost, I said.

Yes, said Agnes, it was an angel fart.

We need fresh air, announced Ross.

He brought us around the side of the barn to a stillborn calf. Bluebottles nestled around the orifices. In the heat the carcass had swelled up like a veiny blue-grey balloon. Ross prodded it with a sharpened stick. He spear-chucked the stick at the bloated stomach. An ungodly stream of thick fluid gushed forth.

Look at it, said Agnes. It's oozing.

Ugh, said Patsy.

What's the matter? It's only a dead calf, said Ross. For emphasis, he poked me in the ribs. I've got way better. I've got a snake pit.

I had learned about the biology of the large and small intestines in school that spring. Unravelled, the adult digestive tract extended for one mile. I imagined mine like a garden hose, the end safely tucked into the toilet bowl. Painfully, methodically, the little bubbles of gas sought the light of day. I doubled over in agony.

Patsy, I'm not up for snakes, I said.

Yeah, but they wiggle, Frannie, she said. It'll be fun. You can cut them.

Please, Ag, let's go home. I'm dying.

Don't be a sissy-fuck, Frannie.

I'm dying.

The snakes lodged writhing under the floor of the collapsing grain silo. Ross chased one until he caught it by the tail. It swirled up, trying to defend itself. He lowered it to the ground, put his foot over the head to hold it down and snapped the snake in two.

Ross! I yelled.

What? It's just a snake.

Yeah, but you don't have to kill it.

The snake vibrated in its death throe.

Nerves is what does that, Ross said.

Agnes whispered, He murdered it.

Patsy said, Murderer, murderer.

The animal stilled in Ross's hand. He flung it away.

Forget it, I've got something better.

Ross McDowell was the pied piper, and Patsy and Agnes were at his mercy. Nothing could stop them. I begged.

Agnes, I have to go.

Can't you go in the woods?

Aggie, please.

Go behind a tree. We won't look.

I followed them, trudging behind the cattle barn, past the yelping, restrained and straining beagles, over a stone fence and through bracken and bramble, canes ripping my skin. Try as I might to suppress the farts, the odd bubble slipped uncontrollably down and shot out the sphincter.

God Almighty, Frannie! said Ross.

Don't swear, I said.

Then don't fart.

Father forgive him, I whispered.

Ross stopped short at the edge of the woods and turned around to face us. He jammed his fist into his trouser pocket and pulled out a polished white fang.

Wolf, he said, and pulled out another.

Let me see those, said Agnes.

Me, me, said Patsy.

He stuck them in his mouth, grimaced and ran at me.

I vant to zuck yore blawd, he said, Ha. Ha. Ha. Ha. Then he

fell down hard, laughing, and rolled onto a patch of stinging nettle, screeched, jumped up and lunged for me again. He overcame me and, by way of pinning me, nestled the fangs into my neck. He ground his pelvis into mine. He must have that sharpened stick in his trouser pocket, I thought. Patsy pushed at him.

Get offa her. Get off.

Agnes said, You're naughty. I'll tattle to your daddy.

Ross McDowell slid off me. His hair was smoky, black with dust, and it skewed out from his head. He slipped into the cedar woods as if through an unlit doorway.

Do you girls want fangs or not?

We stepped in. The floor of the forest was speckled with brown puffball mushrooms. Only dapplings of sun could filter through the dense ceiling. Decay had formed a spongy, dark floor. I shivered.

It was the skeleton of a hound, disobedient or rabid or old, shot and dragged back here. The teeth were carious, black, brown, yellow. Ross McDowell's dad dragged dead animals to the back of the property by way of disposal. The carcasses eased their way into the soil by degrees, by worm and weather, until a mere outline, the skeleton, remained.

Why doesn't he bury them? We always bury our barn cats. Why doesn't he? said Patsy.

That's a stupid waste of time, said Ross.

We hold funerals with candles and prayers, said Agnes. It's not at all stupid.

It's lovely, I said.

Patsy said, Did he drag Grampa McDowell back here, too, when he died of stroke?

Ross growled at her.

I only wanted a private tree, discreet, downwind. My skin tingled hot and ached. A pulsing, insistent need to evacuate sent me off in search of a calm place. The cedar I eventually found grew out of three stems and was russet red. Stringy bark along its surface would make good wipe, and I could hide behind the tree's generous lower boughs. I shimmied my underpants down to my ankles and squatted. It was a plague, a stream from my brown flower, an unstoppable liquid pestilence. I endured its taking leave of me, and when it ended, I was only vaguely better.

My underclothes and skirt were filthy, splattered with cack — a devilish cack of unmistakable smell. I could see my sisters and Ross McDowell as shadows, huddled over the skeleton, leaning in and tugging back furiously. Agnes held up a fang triumphantly. They would finish and begin looking for me. I could not rejoin them. I had suffered enough.

A huge granite slab presented itself, gaped open and invited me to hide beneath it. I crouched there, shivering, while Patsy, Agnes and Ross called and worried and eventually faded away. I cupped my aching head in my sweaty palms. My skin alternated cold and hot, cold and hot. I surrendered to this internal storm, rose and fell at its will for eternity. I would die, I knew. My spirit would look upon my cadaver and lucidity would be mine.

I must have slept. A something, an apparition, its form noble, hung in midair before me.

Who are you? I said.

Don't worry, she said. She was bathed in a blue light and draped in a yellow gown. She didn't *have* a halo so much as she *was* a halo.

What do you want?

It's okay, she said. Really.

All right, I said.

For the longest time she hovered there, looking exactly like the plaster statue in our church but without that little cream-coloured pedestal. She was pensive. Benign. A look of disgust brewed, tangling her forehead. I silently vowed never again to neck with Ross McDowell, and then she spoke.

You tell that boy to go to church, she said.

Are you the Virgin Mary or something?

Is that important?

Yes, I think it might be.

Then I am.

And you want Ross McDowell to go to church? He does.

I want him in our church.

You want me to convert Ross McDowell?

Consider it your vocation.

Not easy, I muttered.

She was gone. Like that. I crept out from my little crevice to look for a weeping tree, a spontaneous Holy Spring, anything, any little verification. I found only my splattered clothes. I balled them up, scratched out a shallow grave and buried them. As I worked, my bowel began to rumble again and my skin to ache. Exhausted, I crawled back under the stone and stared along the forest floor. Wood lice scuttled, ants shifted food and soil, worms undulated in and out like little bits of lost skin. They moved to the rhythm of my breathing.

So alive, I murmured. I felt my organs suffocating.

My eyes fluttered. Then the sensation of rising and falling, of being picked up and then lowered. The outline of my mother's face, starched hairdo, owlish glasses reflecting the light back into my eyes, turtleneck sweater, concern.

Honey, she said. Hi.

Mum.

What happened?

I saw the Virgin Mary, Mum.

Oh, darling, said Mum. It's okay. Really.

Black damaged umbrella; it was Father Bart who loomed over my dead body, blandly administering the sacrament of Extreme Unction. With his index finger, he formed a cross in the air. Agnes and Patsy wept as they stood beside my body, their shapes receding as I dissipated into the atmosphere. They wore new necklaces, beautiful silver chains upon which hung shiny white dog fangs. A sweet gasp and I was no more.

I could only watch while two men dressed in green wrapped my body in plastic and hoisted me into a plush-lined coffin. The upholstery smelled of new car, I of formaldehyde. The casket lid was shut and fastened. The box was lowered into the ground and left there, dirt-covered and cold, to await a dusty future.

This final languor was not to be, of course. The topsoil bled.

Various miracles occurred, attributed to me. The blind saw. The sick sang. The wealthy gave. The poor prospered. And so, too, shovels shifted earth. Workmen swore in the heat. The little immutables of the living — dentures, brass crucifixes, cherished baubles made from plastic, pharmacy-bought reading glasses, black, the lenses gone — were sifted with the soil and redistributed. The casket rose and warmed in the hot summer sun. Out of the coffin my rotting corpse came, out of the polyethylene bag, out into the world and onto a sanctified table. It was inspected, decreed worthy.

The faithful flocked to me and took from me little relics — a tuft of hair, a scrap of my brittle dress, a little scab of dehydrated skin — and placing these in their precious lockets, they thanked, genuflected, kissed and left. The skeleton was sawed, packaged for sale. The rest was saved and a crypt built around it for posterity. Oh, very little remained. Yet still in droves the faithful came, among them the familial and familiar. Ross McDowell bowed. He prostrated himself, and on his knees he approached and kissed the wooden slab on which I lay. He kissed the forehead of my skull. He reached into my mouth, in through the hardened decay of mouth, grabbed my tooth and pulled.

The End of the Line

I.

This was before the electricity went in. Nick and I had bought the land from an old potato farmer by the name of Roch Presley, who claimed to be a distant relative of Elvis. He supplemented his family's income like his papa had, digging grave holes for all the area boneyards, sharing the work with his cousin, enough to go around. We had built living quarters in the eighty-year-old mansard barn, relocating several thousand brown bats and a covey of pigeons. We left the cattle stalls *in situ* on the main floor and framed up the loft, insulated and drywalled, leaving the mortise-and-tenon framework exposed. It was a pretty thing. We were saving to have the Hydro come in and lay a line. Seven grand.

I was pumping ice-cold water from the well into a large plastic bin full of boiled soapy diapers. I wondered how Catharine Parr Traill got hers clean. Mine had greasy-looking orange stains no matter how I scrubbed them. I had Oscar on my back, in a green canvas and aluminum carrier. Warm condensation rose around us.

Oh well, he's just going to shit in them again, anyway. I said this to myself. Oscar was asleep and Nick was in town, putting up a fancy garden fence for a city dweller who likely hadn't the time to sit in his yard anyway — a privacy fence, the lattice work inspired by Japanese architecture. A team of gardeners had been hired to place native plants in natural-appearing settings so the owner and his guests would get the sensation of having just arrived in some untouched boreal forest. This would be tweaked regularly for effectiveness, to give the garden authenticity.

To the north of me was a field abandoned these many years, grown up with pine saplings and alder, black-eyed Susan, valerian, daisy, clover, strawberry, plantain, and various other plants that I could not yet identify. To the south was the barn, a hay field, a vegetable garden and the driveway upon which, as I watched, a white, rusted Camaro now drove. It was caked in mud along the bottom and sported a film of sand everywhere else. The road here was not gravelled but merely laid with sand once a year by the municipality, and so in spring you had to drive through a quagmire at top speed or you were sunk; you had to gun it — blue smoke the entire way. I watched the driver's door clunk open and a slight young man with a three-day beard, a silver and turquoise belt buckle, slim-fit jeans, cowboy boots and jean jacket pop out. His teeth were spaced with little gaps all along like a child's; he was grinning broadly. I should have guessed then but I did not. I had expected it to be my nearest neighbour, Patrice, who had talked about getting a car last time I had seen him prowling along the concession, his rifle slung over his sheepskin veston. There were all types living in the backwoods around Plantagenet. All manner of uncivilized renegades. Patrice was harmless — reckless but honourable, a sort of protector once he'd decided to like you. But this was not Patrice, and it took me some moments to readjust to the facts as they were.

I'm the newcomer, he announced. I'm new.

He was a dead ringer for a man I'd briefly involved myself with down south in Texas — a one-night, well, two-night stand, years ago; I'm not proud of it. I don't remember the man's name, just the facile smile, the belt buckle as it slid down his legs and the feeling of moral abandon as he stripped away my Catholic School upbringing. I had gone down there on a cheap spa retreat with a girlfriend but found I couldn't stand her once I got there. It was stand-by for two amoral days before I caught a flight home.

The memory of it drew down into my body in obvious and distracting ways. I had not had these particular sensations since my pregnancy (when the term libidinous took on a new, improved meaning). Since then, these past months, the baby, the engorged breasts, the flabby residual flesh, the over-charged realigning hormones had pretty much quelled my sexual appetite. But now, here was something — an inappropriate twinge. And as if he could read my mind, this man before me stared deep into my eyes, took a step toward me.

I live in that split log house just up, the last house on the line, he said.

I'm sorry about your wife, I said, for now I knew who this man must be. It was Simon Eliot, from down the concession.

We're managing, he said. Then I noticed his children nestled together on the passenger seat of the car — a boy and a girl. The girl was sucking her thumb.

You're familiar, he said. I've seen you before.

Really?

It was that fleeting time of the year after the snow melted and before the insects lifted out of the earth like spectres and started biting. This was the first winter Nick and I had lived here, even if it was the fifth we'd owned the place. We had been half-time back-to-the-landers until now, moving back and forth to Europe to avoid the bad weather, the lack of paying work. Pretty well everyone around here eked out a bare subsistence, and this had been the worst winter, in terms of snowfall and cold, for forty years. Nick and I endured like backward, unprepared pioneers.

Why the hell would anyone want to colonize this godforsaken land? Nick had bellowed. It was barely reclaimed swampland, sold for a song to disenfranchised French settlers a hundred and fifty years before; the English soldiers got the high ground, but even then there was nothing but rocky soil for tuber growing. And bogs nurturing mosquitoes. The real question was, why did Nick and I colonize it? Nostalgia? Blind aesthetics? We'd fallen for the land in August, on a windy, bug-free day. It was Oscar who, after all, had made us want to settle down, choose a landscape.

I sloshed the diapers around in the bin, drained the water downhill of the well and hauled them around the back of the barn to the clothesline. Simon followed like a puppy beside me; the children peered through the windshield. The boy began to honk the horn — gently pulsing a message to his dad. Simon stuck his index finger in the air.

I'll be back in a minute, he called.

I sat down on the little stoop, built so that I could reach the clothesline, and began wringing out each diaper until I had a stack of them. I could feel a thickness of sorrow around me, making me speechless. I could not place this man, what he wanted with me, what he sought here, how could I help? There wasn't any hindsight later, either; Simon was unreadable. I'd seen Roch filling in the wife's grave. I should have guessed — still waters and all that.

Nick wants to ask you for your contractor's name, I said. We got the go-ahead from Ontario Hydro.

We'll be at either end of the grid, he said.

It's a small world, I said.

The sun was still pretty low at this time of the year, but I hoped its rays would bleach the stains out of these damn diapers. It was embarrassing to see that line of dingy yellow streaks hanging limp in the air above our heads. I could always buy bleach, but I didn't like the idea of contaminating the water table.

Your kids are out of diapers, I suppose, by now, I said.

I don't miss it, either.

It occurred to me that it might be like that all through life — that you strove and achieved and then were thankful it was over with. I felt like that about the birth. When it was over I had, along with a seven-and-a-half-pound baby, delight and a residual resentment against all womankind for not telling the truth about the pain, a profound relief that it was over, forever. Was ambition a sort of addiction to that relief?

I've got bread fresh out, I said. You're welcome to come up. I bake once a week — I have a table at the farmer's market where I sell organic bread.

The children were out of the car by then, playing with the pump, water splashing all over their sneakers and up their legs. You'd expect a bit of laughter, but there wasn't any. They didn't seem unhappy, though — just full of wonder at the device, which they'd clearly never seen before, and an admiration for the magic of pushing a lever and creating a waterfall. Oscar woke up and gurgled at them.

The barn smelled of dust and straw, old cow pats and pigeon droppings. The boards were worn down along the stalls, where the cattle had rubbed away at the cluster flies that must have harassed them in those days. There were no cattle now, no livestock at all. In the winter, Nick and I had stripped out boards for kindling. We were lousy pioneers; the winter came sooner than expected. We had very little dry wood. There was no money, either. We scavenged the forest for deadfall and sawed it up, carrying it back on a makeshift sled: two-by-fours and a sheet of plywood, fixed to a thick yellow rope which we tied to ourselves and pulled on snowshoes to the barn.

The door to the loft was an insulated homemade affair cut into the floor and counter-weighted on the inside with a hunk of granite from a road construction site. The dynamite hole was intact, so we strung it up over an old wooden pulley attached to the ceiling beam and tied the end to the door handle. Clunk — the door was open.

Home sweet home, I said. The sun shone slanting through the loft windows, and the drywall was finally all in and painted right to the roof peak, some thirty feet up. Simon stood in the middle of the place and stared up. His kids spotted the little tractor and replica barn set we'd made for Oscar and began to play. I let the baby out of the backpack, and he flopped about on the floor, gradually moving closer to the children and their game. The pungent smell of rye flour, yeast and chocolate was an almost unbearable enticement. I put the kettle on for tea and sliced one of the little flour-dusted miniature breads, spread it thickly with butter, handed a piece to Simon.

Eat, I said, eat. The bread was a specialty of mine.

Uh, thanks.

Nick and I made everything we could by ourselves. We knew a dairy farmer who was willing to thwart the quota legislation and sell us unpasteurized milk, and with it we made butter, cheese, whipped cream. We had kept chickens through the summer for eggs and had eaten poultry through the winter (I chopped their heads off; we kept the birds in a friend's freezer). We put vegetables and foraged wild fruit by and made ointments of dubious quality using remedy recipes and faith. We dried herbs and mint for tea. Self-sufficiency became a kind of egoistic challenge to which we rose with very little irony. We were tapping several maple trees with the intention of boiling the sap for syrup. We were thinking of keeping goats and making feta and chèvre. The hydro was on its way, and we were moving into the twentieth century. It turned out to be the last year we would live in the country.

Your place is amazing, Simon said. It's fantastic.

I said, I have to put on the generator every now and again and climb a ladder up to the peak window to vacuum up the cluster flies and the bluebottles. I had to buy an extension cord to reach up there.

I wish Kate could have seen this, he said. She grew up in Chalk River, near the nuclear station. A lot of people from around there are riddled with cancers now — leukemia, skin cancer, prostate — little holes form around their noses. They run underground bomb tests and such.

What?

Everyone says that, he said. I don't know why I mentioned it. She would have loved this house, though. His eyes were roaming the ceiling.

After Simon and his children left, I took a walk with Oscar across the road into the Larosse forest. This land had been farmers' fields fifty years ago, but the Ministry of Natural Resources had reclaimed it and planted red pine, which was all the rage for house-framing back then. No one'll touch it now, of course, all that full-grown timber. Everyone wants white pine. Who ever heard of red pine? The canopy let dappled light through where little fairy rings sprouted up in the fall. We never ate the mushrooms, although they looked harmless enough. The undergrowth was minimized by the thick mat of pine needles glowing rust red in the diffused light; the odd fiddlehead fern unfurled there.

It was dry; the trees had sucked up the swamp here forcing the moose deeper into the woods. Small randy herds of them roamed across our property from time to time, escaping from the mosquitoes or crossing from one swamp to the next. The baby reached out to them. Moose are tick-laden, I am told; one must be cautious of Lyme Disease in these parts. I once pulled a burrowing tick out from Oscar's back — the minuscule red-brown legs flailed out of the egg before I crushed it. I sat down on a log to nurse Oscar. The melting patches of snow that the sun could not reach were marvellous. I'd seen snow in June tucked under logs, hiding from the weather. Oscar had sucked holes into my nipples. I flinched when he latched on, as the healing sores reopened.

When Nick drove up the lane that night, I did not immediately tell him about Simon's visit, although it was all I could think about. I pulled the ripcord on the generator and calibrated the instantaneous water heater, ran the shower until the air within the plastic curtain steamed. Oscar was asleep in the cedar cradle Nick had hand-hewn from green wood and pieced together. We ate our dinner as the lights soaked the last bit of energy from the car battery we had rigged up. I lit a kerosene lamp and three candles, and we sat across the table from each other, our pupils dilated, like rabbits transfixed by sudden headlights. It was ten o'clock when I got up to do the dishes.

He came by today, the guy whose wife died.

Did you ask him about the hydro?

I told him you wanted to talk to him. He was sad.

I wouldn't mind seeing that house he built.

He seemed kind of needy. I guess that's normal.

Like needy what? said Nick.

I dunno.

I was up three times in the night with Oscar. When I changed his diaper, his fingers reached for his penis. Babies seek comfort in their own bodies as soon as they are able. I lit a candle and tried to nurse him to sleep. I noticed that his eyes were changing from the bottomless blue of every baby to something inquiring — a person was emerging. I still felt I didn't know him; he was a stranger in our midst, forcing transformation. Besides, I was thoroughly sleep-deprived, unable to form, to assemble cohesive or reasonable, examinable thoughts. I wafted through the days as they wafted through me. Motherhood had severed me from myself in inscrutable ways. Nick pulled me over to him in the morning.

I said, I can't. I just can't.

I was so tired I could not rightly function. After Nick left for work, I took the camper van we had bought while working on the barn, and I drove it through byways, passing time. I liked the lazy yaw of it, the rocking, the soporific nothing of it. Near Wendover, I was forced to brake for two annoyed turkey vultures, who opened their wings and spanned the road, protecting their mangled feast. My heart rose at their ungodly beauty. They were eating roadkill — crushed groundhog — pulling strands of intestine up, tearing, tearing. It did not disgust me; it fascinated me. The viscera of life was worth observing, perhaps obsessing over. Childbirth was all spilling, too; it was the offal of life — the placenta (that island of sustenance), the coil of umbilicus, the waters, blood, the unexpected defecation at the eleventh hour. Placenta interests doctors and cosmetic manufacturers, too. One sells it; the other buys it. Think of that next time you apply lipstick. And even though we kept it, had the doctors refrigerate it, and even though we eventually buried it under a rosebush, it would still have a use to some colony of insects scuttling underground. It is the culinary that draws me, the culinary and the sexual; these form the separation of birth and death. They provide the everything in between.

Simon came by again. I saw him through the porthole window we had made under the eaves. He came walking, three dishevelled, mixed-breed hounds rallying around him, nipping and yapping.

They crowded in on me when I came down, nestling their cold snouts into my crotch.

Cut that out, Mimi, he said. Silky, no.

They're just dogs, I said. What's up?

Just walking.

The kids?

Windsor. I brought them to their grandparents. I gotta go looking for work, now. Ah, I'm in no shape. There's the boxes still to unpack. We never did have a chance to move in.

Come in a sec. I have to change Oscar again. Christ, he's prolific.

I used my head to push the trap door open and took Oscar over to the change table, a blanket box, really. He had wet through his rubber pants, and the milk urine had soaked through his sleeper and into my sweatshirt. I pulled off his clothes. His penis was wildly erect; a stream of pee arced through the air.

Ach, no. Again.

Well endowed, the little bugger.

He'll do okay.

The dogs were whining outside, occasionally barking when they could stand their own whines no longer. I could hear one of them scrambling at the door, drawing its claws down the wood. It didn't matter, it wasn't a good door or anything.

I brought some papers from the hydro, he said. You'd maybe do better with solar, I dunno.

There isn't enough sun. I did some research there.

There's too much cloud cover?

That's what I heard. Too expensive. We can't . . .

The dogs were baying now and moving away from the house toward the road. They were warning of something. I went to the peephole window. I felt self-conscious; this showed something about what I did when I was nervous, that I needed a peephole view, that I was paranoid. It was Patrice coming up the lane. He had his jeans tucked into a pair of natural leather wooden-soled boots, mid-calf, he wore a handwoven vest edged in fur of some sort, maybe raccoon, and his rifle was strapped across his back.

His stringy, blond-grey hair was tied back in a thin braid. He kicked
the dogs off him. When I turned around, Simon was smiling.

That's Patrice checking up on you.

Yes, I guess he heard the dogs, I said.

Patrice was yelling, Stupid, fucking chiens. Allo? Any body
there?

It's okay, Patrice, I called down. Simon Eliot and his dogs are
by with information on the hydro.

Ah, fuck, he said. Hurry up and get it so I can make some
toast at my place, too.

I watched Patrice look up at the barn. He put his hand to his
forehead; for a minute I thought he was going to cross himself.
He rubbed his hands down his chest, then turned and walked
back down the drive. One of Simon's dogs ran and nipped at his
ankle and barked the whole way. I believe it would have followed
him home had Patrice not fired a warning shot into the air.
Patrice lived in a series of broken-down school buses along a labyrinth of mowed paths in the depth of a young spruce forest. He
moved from one bus to the next as the mood struck him. None
of them had what anyone normal would consider amenities. The
dog squealed and hurried back to its mates.

I'm getting rid of the dogs, if you want one, said Simon.

It might be nice, I said.

Well, here's those papers. The contractor was fair, I guess, if
they ever are.

I put Oscar in the wheelbarrow that afternoon, padded him
in with a tartan wool blanket and several stuffed animals. I put
the small 0-34 Stihl in there, too, and went down to the bush to
fell some little dead maple trees I'd seen. We were still firing up
the woodstove by night, and so we were again low on fuel. Red
and white trilliums urged up through the earth, unfurling their
thick, waxy leaves. Orchids, with their translucent human-like
veins, gaped like organs out of the brown, leafy decay. I worked
slowly, stopping the chainsaw whirr frequently so as not to upset
the boy and gathering the wood into the bottom half of the
wheelbarrow, leaving space for Oscar. The birds, of course, were

silent. Forest creatures are mortally afraid of people. Even chipmunks scurry off in terror at the slightest human rustle. Was it our size or our innate intention? I, too, felt something like fear alone in the forest; the animals were assessing me.

Oscar and I spent the rest of the afternoon on a couple of sheepskins, lolling under the roiling sky. An early spider was spinning up a triangle of grass blade near us; I watched her twang the cord, music-making, moving a strand down, weaving her net. There would be thunder and cracking lightning that evening. In the morning, we stared in wonderment across the open field. Every spider had spun in the night; a thousand thousand webs receded on the plain. It was an infinity of arachnoid hopes catching dew, possibly dinner. I had not told Nick about Simon's visit. It was the spiders that somehow reminded me.

He brought by the paperwork, I said.

Who?

The neighbour. He came by with his hounds. He left his contractor's papers for you.

I should get over there, Nick said.

II.

The last time I saw Simon was a bread-making day, a Friday. I'd left several heaps of sour desem dough rising on the table. I was taking a break and had filled our old claw foot bathtub. The water was almost too warm to get into, but I had done it anyway. Oscar was with me, standing splashing outside the bath, and when Simon called out from the front of the barn, I frantically pushed the water droplets off my skin as I lifted out of the tub and tugged on my T-shirt dress. People shouldn't drop by unexpectedly. There was no time. I hoped he wouldn't gape at my postpartum belly, swollen milk-filled breasts, at the mess I felt myself to be in.

Hang on, I yelled too late.

He said, Oh, sorry.

I said, No, I'm baking for market tomorrow. I just needed a break, you know?

I pulled my apron over my head and strapped it twice around my waist. I had picked up Oscar, and he was pulling at my shirt, running his pudgy hand over my nipple, leaning into me, his mouth askew, seeking to suck. Simon gaped.

Ah, fuck, I said. I unstrapped the apron and sat down on a splitting stump set out in one of the old stalls. I pulled down the dress and stuck Oscar to my breast. He made the most awful sucking noises. Blue and red vessels beneath the skin, conduits one never notices before motherhood, seemed to pulse as he sucked. A certain anxiety that builds as milk is produced and stored in the glands dissipated as he pulled it down into himself. I felt calm.

What's up with you? I said.

I was walking, he said, thought I'd stop in.

Oh, yeah. No work.

I haven't been able to work.

I switched Oscar over to the other side. His eyes were closing drunkenly. It was nap time. I slipped my pinkie into his mouth to break the seal he had formed on me. Then I brought him upstairs; he had outgrown his cradle and now slept on a futon on the floor next to ours. Simon had followed us.

I keep hoping to run into your husband, he said.

Weekends, I said, weekends he'll be out felling along the line. It's scheduled, the hydro, for the end of May. We went with a different contractor than you, someone cheaper.

Oh, weekends, no. I go to the kids. I go to Windsor.

It's lucky you have that support.

I guess that's luck.

I could see the dough was close to rising over, the yeast would run out of nourishment. I punched three of the overgrown heaps down and kneaded them up into taut balls to rise again. The fourth I began to cut into half-kilo slabs. The dough sighed — a pungent acidic wheat release. This bread made on the edge of its possible timing would rise in the oven; it would be light and even in texture. Simon leaned into me and grabbed my hand. He pulled me over toward him; the dough I clutched as he did this was damaged beyond hope; he kissed me lightly alongside my mouth.

I said, Hey.

He said, I watch you from the bush most days. I follow you into the forest when you go gathering firewood and flowers. I watch the moose watch you. You remind me . . .

Simon.

You're safe with me. You don't need to worry about anything when I am around.

I just wanted you to know. I'm here to help you.

I don't need you to watch me, I said. You have to stop doing it.

If I don't watch you . . . it's so painful, if I don't watch you. You have no idea.

Go home, Simon. This is weird. You know it, too.

Nick and I discussed plans to call in the police, to call the municipality, to call the nut house, to organize some community aid with Patrice, Roch and some of the other neighbours, to convene and intervene in a way that might help Simon or keep him away from me. We did nothing, of course, but months later we moved away, lured by sure work and the easy city life, a job in Toronto.

What did he do then, Nick said, after he grabbed your arm? I don't much like that, by the way. Some guy grabbing your arm. Maybe you shouldn't have been breastfeeding in front of him.

Well, sure, I said. The baby was hungry. I didn't know he was stalking me.

Stalking you, I never thought of that, he said. So, what did he do?

He started to cry, and then he said goodbye and left.

The bread was stacked loaf on loaf along the entire oaken table. I took a loaf and cut a few thin slices from it. We ate bread and cheese that night and climbed into bed early. Oscar climbed all over Nick and laughed as Nick gently tossed him up and caught him. And as the boy grew hungry, Nick settled him into my arms, helping him to find the nipple.

You are a little nothing, Nick said. Oscar looked up at him. I leaned over and kissed Nick, ran my hand down his chest, tugged my fingers through his pubic hair.

What's this?

I don't know, I just feel like it.

Finally, he said.

We did not know it yet, but thousands of mosquitoes had hatched that day. As we made love, they were pushing through tiny holes we had not properly caulked, pushing hungrily into the dying afternoon heat of our barn. They would begin to swarm our sweet-smelling skin before we could, before even Nick's belt buckle could slide down his legs and I could lose myself in that fantasy.

Dead Man's Sheets

The bed sheets were ancient, with a thread count of now unseen magnitude, and bleached a blinding, virginal white, at least on cursory inspection. They were twisted along the bed and about the arms and legs of Sam and Mira. People have hanged themselves from bedsheets or escaped by tying them together end on end like a primitive ladder. Sam and Mira will not escape, they will climb neither up nor down, but more likely remain in the stasis that has marked their relationship from the outset — a sort of symbiosis that, while appearing benign or even (some say) kindred from afar, is analogous to a mutual parasitism, a relationship in which the participants, simple, single-celled, slowly devour one another.

Mira bought the bedsheets. Fine, crisp percale sheets are so satisfying to the eye, especially in summer when one longs for coolness. She didn't notice the unidentifiable stain until she shook them out over the blue steel bedstead. It was a smallish oblong of sepia coloration that appeared to have been gone at with a scrub brush and a bleach concentrate, to no avail. The threads were worn and slightly damaged in that area. It stood to reason that the sheets were flawed. Mira had picked them up for a song at a garage sale, and while she wasn't surprised to discover the stain, she was appalled. It signified something tainted or unsavoury, something one wouldn't want associated with one's bed. She turned the sheet around so that the stain would be hidden at the foot of the bed, on her side, and she folded the corners over the futon mattress. Then she changed the pillow cases and the top sheet and stood back. The stain showed through the second layer.

How annoying.

She wouldn't tell Sam. She covered the offending area with an old quilt, accordion folded across the end of the bed. Sam and Mira were nearing the end of the initial golden period of a relationship, that six to seven week period when traditionally couples feel themselves special, invincible and somehow united. A desperate inseparability had set in that they began to cultivate as if it were love. It might have been love.

Somehow in their sexual intercourse the night before, the flat sheet had twisted along the top half of the bed, through her legs and along his neck, so that only their feet and part of their calves were covered. It didn't much matter; it was that hot in the apartment. The sex had sated them, which wasn't saying much, since she was young and he was undersexed (self-described). It was a missionary-style event with no real deviations. This transpired, roughly, at three a.m. after a lengthy conversation that took various unexpected turns, leading Sam to divulge information about himself — his tendency to violence; his adoration of his father, who, in a depressed state had quit his job as a pharmacy clerk and armed all his able-bodied sons (three) and organized them into a mini-mob, robbing small grocery stores, medical supply outlets, Taco Bells etc.; and his first intercourse (age twelve) with a likewise pre-pubescent girlfriend — truths that he had vowed never to reveal. Mira had a knack for exposition and may have missed her calling as a journalist to pursue a half-time career in old books.

She worked in a dust-accumulating antiquarian bookstore called Tomes, located conveniently in the room below her apartment. The store was underlit and badly organized; stacks of old books and brittle ephemera lay behind the front desk in mounds, awaiting identification and classification, pricing. There was a small table of publishers' overstock, books with offensive black Magic Marker swipes along the top edges, or discarded review copies, and a metal book display which could be spun in search of that highly sought-after Harlequin romance or one of those garish sex and crime novels that cater to the Everyman — books that the Quaker store owners held in contempt but that, nevertheless, were the bread and butter of their small business. Mira ran the till, assessed and priced incoming stock, arranged the window display seasonally, shelved and alphabetized and, for the rest, maintained an erudite atmosphere by reading large, dusty, leather-bound editions behind the counter. She was a student of literature at the University of Ottawa, which seemed to her a failure of ambition, even though it was the only university that would have her out of the three to which she'd applied. She hadn't really tried to achieve much in her final year of high school; this she found to be a mitigating factor in terms of self esteem.

Sam laid bricks, specialized in interlock. He was a renegade, a fan of Marty Robbins (most notably "El Paso") and John Mayall (the vocal gibberish especially), he was a thief, a slow study and possibly an assassin. He wasn't particularly good looking, although he had soft, downy chest hair and, when erect, a formidable member. His one manly claim to fame, the obvious notwithstanding, was his gentle and unassuming outward nature, the air of mystery that he had developed to create a bit of allure. He was heterosexual; however, he saved his true self for familial relationships — father, mom, three brothers and two sisters. Whatever Sam felt for others was lesser, suspect and volatile. He was born south of the Mason-Dixon line and damned proud of it.

I see someone, Mira said. Exhausted, she had just surfaced from a near-sleep state. Sam was saying something that she couldn't make sense of. She could see him sitting up in bed, the skin of his stomach rippled where his torso bent. He was inhaling the smoke from a mentholated Craven A in a way that suggested meditation or divinity, peppermint flavoured. He said something louder and to her.

Who is it?

I don't know him, she said. He's not the dead guy, not the

guy you killed. This one is fat, obese really, and is struggling with his breath. He is choking.

He is sitting or he is standing?

He is sitting. He is very fat and turning blue. His eyes are popping. Maybe he is having a heart attack.

Sam drew on his cigarette. He had a cowboy effeteness to him — slow, sexy, glamorous and nostalgic.

He is old, bald?

Yup.

Is he wearing a damp striped terry cloth towel?

How'd you know that?

At this point Sam was out of bed. He pulled his blue jeans and his boots on and went into the kitchen to the flesh-coloured wall-mounted phone. The yellow kitchen walls looked ash white in the city night glow. Sam dialled 214-243-5121. It took a long time for someone to pick up.

Michael? Get Mom. Yeah. I know. Don't ask, I just do. He ain't having no heart attack though? Yeah? Don't ask, I said. Is he okay, now? Mum okay? Tell her I love her. Yeah. Yeah. I'm doing fine. Any news? No, fuck the newspapers, I mean around. Is there news? Aw, fuck. Michael? Everyone's got . . . yeah? You sleep tight, too. I know what time it is. Yeah, I know. It ain't like that. No, it's just real simple, whatever anybody else says. Don't mess with Texas. Huh? I won't, you know that. Yeah. Yeah. Bye now. Bye.

You're some weird girl, he said when he returned.

Did someone die? Mira said.

Pa was choking on a midnight snack.

Kidding?

I wish.

Mira looked over the edge of the bed and stared dully at the dreadlocked burnt-orange pile carpet matted with cat hair. She did not own a vacuum, though she sometimes felt she lived in one. She watched a flea side hop maniacally along the pile. Mira had been aware of this infestation for some time and had not yet bought a collar for the cat. The orange tabby had been a solution to a mouse problem, but not a particularly good one; she could still hear them scuttling in the walls. She reached out and pinched the flea between the nails of her index finger and thumb and wiped the carcass on the carpet.

Wish what?

Wish you wouldn't refer to my father as fat, obese, etc.

I didn't know he was your father at the time.

The apartment was in the ratty university district of the city, and the buildings were old and dilapidated. Many of the trees had been cut down over the years due to Dutch elm disease and carpenter ant problems. There was still an old pin oak around the corner on Sylvan Ave that was a designated heritage tree and thought to predate all the architecture in the area. Sam and Mira could see it if they crossed over to the corner store and happened to look up.

It was a hot summer. The air was dense with moisture, industrial toxins and car fume fug. Mira found the nights unbearable — thick and dream-filled and horny, always that. She watched Sam toss about in the white sheet until he'd twisted it into a cord and pushed it off the bed. He reeked vaguely of alley, piss, puke and dishonour. Mira got a sublime high from reading Sam's mind, his fortune, his future, and also from the thrill that control offered. She watched his cock come erect in his sleep — he was the only person she had ever known or heard of who could sleep-fuck and have no waking recollection of it. She watched the heart beneath his skin rumble and quit and oblige itself back to life. How often each night did Sam die? she wondered. How often would he come back to life? Mira leaned over and shook him until he grunted and woke up, slurping a short strand of drool back into his mouth. His penis sank down, shrunk to a wrinkled slug.

So what was he wearing? she asked.

Like I said — a blue and red striped terry cloth towel.

No. The dead man.

Why do you have to know all that?

I dunno. You don't have to tell me.

Well, Christ, Mira, Sam said. He liked turquoise. He had on jeans, of course, and a belt with a big turquoise-studded buckle, slicers. The man was a shit kicker. He had these chunky rings, and a plaid fringe shirt. He was a real shit kicker, you understand?

Face up?

Listen Mira, you don't wait until a man is facing you before you kill him. Nobility is for the movies. The guy's for sure got a gun, anyway. Bad enough I did it. I don't want his nasty face on my conscience. Now, quit pestering me, will you?

So. You shoot him in the back. Blood is everywhere, splatter just everywhere. He falls — wham — face down in the desert dust. Or. He falls slow-mo as you realize the awful thing you've done. Which?

The former.

Okay, he's dead, the force of his fall smashes his face into the earth, and in the distance an unconnected siren winds out. You freeze.

I never froze in my life. Take that back.

You ran.

I ran.

His corpse is discovered five days later, by which time you are living under an assumed name in another part of the country. What was his crime? Whose blood is on his conscience?

His crime had not yet been enacted. It was still in the premeditative stage. I saved him from himself. Can you leave me alone now? Mira?

Was the turquoise clear, or was it marbled with black and flecked with gold?

Mira?

Yes?

I'm very unreliable. It might have been amber or onyx.

Not turquoise at all?

I have a bad memory. I'm also very tired.

Sam was captivated by the intimacy that Mira assumed over him. The detail of information that she drew out of him seemed to hold him hostage to an image of himself he didn't necessarily want perpetuated. Yet he cared for her, or convinced himself he cared for her, deeply. Sam felt that Mira was special, preternaturally gifted, although he would never have put it that way. He always called it clairvoyance and urged her to pursue it as a career. It occurred to her too late that she should have jumped his bones while he was sleeping. Now that he was awake and unwilling to play her mind game, she would have to endure boredom, horniness and his insomnia.

You could open a little storefront, start a business, Sam suggested. A business of the mind.

I only suffer it with you, she said.

Think of the people you could help.

You've watched too much day-time TV in your life, Sam.

Yeah, yeah, yeah, think of the talk show circuit, seriously.

You just want to shift the burden off your own shoulders.

Really. You should think about this.

She scrunched up her eyes and said, I see a single mother-fucker hitchhiking south on a lonely interstate highway, tears flowing down his cheeks.

And funny, too, you're a fucking natural, Mira.

His interest in Mira predated, by at least a couple of days, any exhibition of psychic prowess on her part. There was a brief period at the beginning when he was smitten but still incompletely bound. He had the match lit before she had her cigarette to her lips. Mira had a badly permed hairdo, which she had tried but failed to tease into a punk style, and a look of familiarity about the eyes. What had transpired between them was more recognition than love at first sight. In fact, she had an intelligent gleam that should have warned him but didn't.

Sam drank on Fridays. The expectation in the manly world of bricklaying, into which he had been hired under the table and therefore, he claimed, in which he had to fulfill a commensurately higher degree of expectation, was that he would remain after work each Friday and get shitfaced on tepid Canadian beer with his former Nazi boss and his former Nazi boss's son. Being slightly allergic to alcohol and of low body weight, Sam was by anyone's standards a cheap drunk. He also had a heart murmur and had been advised not to drink by several doctors, including the army physician who had declared him unfit. (For service, you mean, sir? No. Just unfit generally.)

Mira asked only twice whether Sam'd been drinking because, by the second week of his living in her apartment, his finding this so-called temporary employment, and his giving the tiresome and unconvincing macho explanation regarding job expectation, it was obvious to her that the situation was unchangeable.

Huh? Uh, yeah. I had a couple. Yeah.

And then, like a cat who has caught the mouse but out of sheer mercenary joy hasn't killed it yet, Mira began to deliver a mild but pointed form of torture that over time she came to call Hurricane.

Tell me about your brother, Mira said. The one who chases the wind.

Wind?

Yeah, cyclone brother.

Did I ever say anything about him before?

I just know, Sam. Tell about the cyclone of 1979.

How it spun.

Mira said, I saw the wind gathering fragments of dead leaves. I saw the earth swirling up its deadfall in accumulating masses of debris.

The look of hunger in my brother's eyes. He longed to follow it. We jumped in his car and drove behind it for miles through the desert. It looked artificial. The velocity of its spin was incredible. It dazed the mind. Cyclone brother . . .

Was he real? Or did you make him up?

Both. He dreamed of finding the centre and holding his spot.

The Oldsmobile, he realized, would be totalled. It was uninsured. He stood there in his seersucker shorts and striped blue and green jersey, hunger palpable on his face.

You see?

Yes.

Oh, God, stop the merry-go-round, Mira, stop.

A poem, Mira announced suddenly. This was her favourite part.

No, please, Mira.

She recited:

> *Oh what a twister*
> *My lovely sister*
> *Gone.*
> *Just sitting on the lawn*
> *I wisht that I misst her*
> *I never did kisst her*
> *Done.*

That's very sad.

Thank you, Sam. Mira repeated the poem several times at breakneck speed until it became in itself a sort of violent wind storm.

Excuse me, Sam said, and stumbled to the toilet. She knew she had won the game when she heard his coughing heaves and the muffled, Oh Christ, and, then, Christ, Mira! that were his only solace there, in the porcelain bowl. The cat sat near him, licking its forepaw, circling this moisture over its face and blinking.

Mira woke with the first caw of the alarm clock, six a.m. She reached over Sam's body and slammed it off.

Sam?

Huh?

Your alarm went off. Are you supposed to work today?

Yeah, uh, thanks.

She prodded him for a few minutes more and then fell back to sleep. The hours slid by, the heat of the day rising to a torpid pinnacle around eleven, and still no sign of life. The phone, which had rung on and off since seven, had given up any possibility of being answered and was silent. The couple were experiencing a driving sleep, a winding, chaotically dream-sullied complication of sleep. In fact, when they awoke and compared their stories, they discovered simultaneous twin dreams. They took this as some sort of love proof.

What time is it?

Oh shit, shit, shit. Damn. The alarm . . .

Went off.

Oh fuck. It's eleven-thirty. I'm, oh fuck, I'm dead.

Just call, make something up. Tell them you, uh, overslept.

They'll fire me. I need a good lie. Oh damn.

Tell them the truth, that you can't drink, you're allergic, I dunno. That you overslept.

It won't work, you don't know these people. They need a lie, a good lie, or they'll fire me.

People like the truth. You overslept. Try that.

Mira, you're not being supportive. The man is an SS.

I thought you said he was a *former* Nazi.

Once a Nazi, always a Nazi.

Well, people do change.

Sam was pulling on his brown gingham country-boy shirt. It had an upside-down wave of white piping across the chest and mother-of-pearl snaps down the front. He shoved his green and white deck of cigarettes into the breast pocket, then pulled it out, opened it, and drew one out for each of them. Technically, no smoking was a condition of renting the apartment, but the land-lords were fairly lenient on such things; being Quakers, they tended to look on the bright side. They had been very welcoming to Sam, especially when they deduced that he was some sort of refugee. Perhaps they acquiesced to the smoking because they felt sorry for him. The mentholated cigarettes were a compromise, Mira's idea, because she felt they didn't smell quite so bad.

I'm illegal, Mira, *illegal*. They'll fire me and not pay me. That's two weeks' free work, and me fired, moping around here, fucked. The future looks gloomy, Mira. I'm going to need a perfect lie, one brimming with testosterone. I need a fist fight, something honourable. I need a black eye, superficial wounds, a limp. As proof.

Proof?

A fight with honour. I was protecting you from slander. That's it. Some asshole whistled, lascivious behaviour, ball grabbing, tongue waggling, someone used the word twat in your direction. I went wild, I cracked. The Nazi will be drawn into the story; they will want details. With my lie, I will attain hero status, possibly a raise.

You're going to punch yourself?

That's where you come in, Mira. Can you get mad? You're taking that theatre course at the university. Get mad, Mira. Punch me. Here in the eye. I want you to punch me, you bitch.

This is noble?

Take this arm, pull back with all your might, and . . . no, make a fist for crying out loud . . . and whack me one, sock it to me. I need you, Mira. You can do this.

I can't do this.

For me.

Mira pulled an oversized tank top on and went out the front door with her smoke to think. The cool night air had burned away; cicadas and air conditioners spun out their summer songs. There wasn't anything to look at but a dry patch of grass and a spindly, hopeless morning glory winding up the low chain-link fence that enclosed the postage-stamp yard. In the bedroom, Sam carefully untwisted the bedsheet, smoothed it as best he could and tucked it under the mattress. When Mira came back inside the house, he was standing in the kitchen, swinging a large cast iron frying pan as if to test it for weight and balance.

You can hit me with this instead if you like, Mira.

I saw the man's children. Mira was churlish and seemed to be elsewhere, as if she was working out a difficult problem to which there might be no solution.

Mira?

A towhead and an auburn.

Mira? What the fuck . . .

They're running around a toy-strewn yard, water pistols, heads are popped off dolls. The sprinkler, old, shoots out a pathetically lopsided stream, the mother stands to one side; she's worried.

Get the hell out of my head, Mira.

Where's Daddy? says the towhead. Oh, he's with the angels, replies the auburn in a squeaky voice. Angels ain't real, says towhead. How did they know?

I got enough already, Mira, quit that.

The man's body puffs, then shrinks, dehydrating in the desert heat. His turquoise belt sinks, heavy, makes a strange indentation into his rotting belly. Sam, tell me, who is not guilty of thinking bad thoughts?

You're fucking with me, Mira, don't fuck with me.

The wife is upset; she thinks he's abandoned her. She has her brothers searching for him. If they find him they aim to hurt him badly, perhaps kill him. One of her brothers likes the idea of killing him, after what he's done, the bastard. But it's too late. You held up your sawed-off shotgun, an idiot could shoot and kill with that, no need to aim, you called out to him plaintively, as if you meant to rekindle a friendship, he half turned . . .

Mira . . .

. . . smiling, his hand shot out to shake yours. Instead, a shock of impact, a burning, the clarity of an image — his boys — and . . .

I'm warning you, Mira.

Sam? Give me that pan.

Mira grabbed it out of his hand. It arced along the yellowish background of the kitchen wall and slammed viciously into him, he grinned recklessly, blood spurted from his nose. His head ricocheted like a cartoon character's, his eyes widened in pain, but his laugh was deep and rich and full-bodied.

Thank you, Mira. You're a fuckin' babe.

Sam spent a great deal of time examining the wound in the bathroom mirror. His face was disappointingly unbruised. He slid the medicine cabinet mirror open, took out a plastic cartridge of razors, and drew one delicately along his cheek, his chin, and slashed his nose. Droplets of blood oozed out quickly, congealing into raw scabs. The smoke from the cigarette clenched in his teeth forced his eyes into a squint that looked fabricated in a cowboy-tough sexy way. It went with the injuries.

You'll have to hit me again, sweetie, he called, his voice thinning as it bounced off various walls before it reached her.

What?

This ain't bruised. There ain't no black eye. Fuckin' headache, but that don't prove nothing.

Sam, that was a one-off. I'm not doing it again. Won't. Can't. This is ridiculous, eh?

What's ridiculous is that I'm asking you to help me and you either aren't receiving the information or you are not interested in this relationship.

Because I don't want to hit you?

Look, Mira, if I could punch myself, I would. I'm fuckin' practically begging here. It's not that hard. You did it once. You can do it again. Just punch me. I need this.

I've never hit anyone in my life, Sam. This isn't easy for me.

You'll thank me for this.

I have to lie down.

The heat was thick in the apartment. Mira lay sprawled on the bed. The cat jumped up and started to knead her back. Purring loudly, dribbling saliva, it kneaded with increasing aggression, pulling up twists f thread and puncturing her skin with its claws. The white garage-sale sheet wicked the sweat from her body, so that later, when she got up, grappled Sam to the floor, punched him repeatedly in the face until the look of controlled pleasure and love-filled wonderment there had turned to dismay and fear and he had pushed her off, not without some effort, the shape of her torso, legs and arms, and the side of her face could be seen as a darkened impression on the bed, as if some part of her still lay there. The cat had nestled into the place where her belly had been and had fallen asleep.

The ruse worked. Sam was not fired. He kept his job, placing one brick atop another or beside, building retaining walls, fancy walkways, bricking up inefficient windows and drinking warmish beer with the boss and the boss's offspring each Friday after work, chuckling at off-colour jokes to maintain the workaday camaraderie and to keep his job. There were repercussions, however, as perhaps there always are. Sam's plan, while securing his position, at least for the time being, unleashed in Mira a heretofore subverted violence. This was inconsequential to Sam initially; in fact, born in Texas, bred in New Mexico, he found her little acts of roughness and occasional brutality, if not par for the course, then at least more natural behaviour than her typical Yankee passivity.

Fell for it, lock, stock and barrel. Guys are f-ing idiots. Sam unhitched his tool belt and let it slip to the floor. He pulled out a fold of paper money from his back jeans pocket and thrust it down on the little IKEA side table in front of Mira. The orange tabby cat recoiled in surprise as the bills scattered over the table and down along the carpet; Mira looked up at Sam in disgust.

There's bacon, girl.

There's what? Bacon?

Mira took the cat by its midsection and hurled it in Sam's general direction. The claws ejected and clung spontaneously to his bare chest, and the now bristle-furred animal hung there momentarily like a stretched skin curing on a wall.

What the hell did you do that for Mira?

What the hell did I do that for? What? Don't throw money at me. Don't do that.

That's three hundred bucks.

The cat pushed itself off Sam's chest and fled screeching toward its litter box. Sam pondered the attack for hours with no real solutions to the questions it raised in his mind, and finally, late in the night, he woke Mira, partly out of frustration at his insomnia and partly to re-establish something he felt had shifted in their relationship.

Why'd you do that, Mira?

I just did it without really thinking, Sam.

You could apologize.

I liked the way the animal twisted and turned midair. I liked the way it found a footing vertically. I could apologize. But I don't feel sorry.

Do you feel anything?

I feel curious. I enjoy the pictures I get in my head when you are around. I enjoy that intensity of image, and the possibility of vision. I like the fear in your eyes when I see things you don't want revealed.

You like hurting me.

That would be an odd way of putting it.

Damn straight, Mira.

She began to draw blood during their lovemaking. She liked to see the lines of their passion drawn onto him as if they contained some important encoded message. Mira's acts of violence were nonetheless inconclusive. Sam felt they were separate incidents and as such could be explained away. She was excited; she was angry. He liked the tension of possibility between them now; there was comfort there. Once, during an argument that she had unfairly precipitated concerning how she could truly gauge Sam's love for her, in which he had uttered several if not unkind then certainly nonchalant placations, Mira had fallen into a rage, thrown off her down-filled coat, stripped away every stitch of clothing, thrown these at him, and stood there in the middle of an abandoned parking lot screaming at the top of her lungs into the night.

Fucker! You fucker!

January in Ontario is very cold; Sam bundled her up and took her back to the apartment. He laid her down along the electric floor radiator and heaped Hudson's Bay blankets over her shivering body.

Thank you, Sam. I love you, you know that, don't you?

Sure, Mira, I know that.

Her temperature rose and fell through the night, and he dutifully pulled the blankets on and off, lying awake, smoking, listening to the soft drawl of Loretta Lynn inciting heartbreak in the background, fighting an erection that had inexplicably inhabited him and applying cold compresses to Mira's burning forehead and neck. Mira muttered unintelligible phrases and occasionally moaned. Then, weirdly, her eyes opened wide, then shut, and she slept. When she woke up the skin around her eyes seemed translucent with new baby arteries, blue, visible beneath the flesh.

I've been watching you all night.

Mira just stared out at him. You've been there all along watching me.

Yeah, Mira, all through the night. You feeling any better?

The dead man with the turquoise belt has sunk into near nothingness, Mira said to him then. Birds have done what birds do, the weather has taken care of the rest. A jumble of sun-bleached cloth holds the vague shape of the man as it hangs about the ribcage, but even that has been softly buried by shifting sands, and desert seeds eager to take hold. His wife has met another man, and although she feels a horny thrill of guilt as he pulses in and out of her most nights, her rancour at what she perceives as abandonment has subsumed into gratefulness to this new fellow who gets on with the boys and seems to revel in his newfound role as father/protector/lover. Her brothers have left off their hunt.

Mira said this all in a monotone, as if in a trance, and then that week she brought home books on torture she'd found hidden in a box in the bookstore bathroom. *The History of the Rod*, *The History of Torture Throughout the Ages*, *Colour Atlas of Neuropathology* (pastel photographs of disease-tortured brain cells), *The Art of Flower Arrangement* (the torture of plants). Clearly, the Quakers had not known what to do with these violent books, even how to categorize them. Or possibly they felt it better for humanitarian reasons to withhold them from the general public. Mira began to take an unhealthy interest in the local wastrels that came into the store, particularly the psychopath who ran his face along staple-pocked telephone poles ripping little holes into his flesh in repeated attempts to match inside with out. He would come into the store sometimes and buy obscure books on the

Queen Mother and bicker with himself. She tried to touch him when she handed him back his change.

Atone, he said.

What?

He stared at her fiercely. Never mind, he blurted.

Mira's sleep fractured, most nights just shards of dream and nothing. She lay awake and looked over the books by the bed, fascinated by the etchings of early crucifixions, bare-bottomed floggings, impalings, burnings at the stake, the plaques and tangles of severely demented brain cells and the cruel wire reinforcement of weak anemone stems. She shifted and tossed until the cat leapt off the bed and Sam woke up and reached for a smoke, and then she would harass him. She was bored and lonely and fixated.

Why'd you do it?

What?

Kill the man with the turquoise belt.

You woke me up for this? I'm tired. Let me alone . . .

Did you hate him? Were you angry?

Mira, I was curious, okay? I liked the way his body twisted and turned before he fell to the ground.

It pleased you to see his pain.

That's an odd way of putting it, Mira.

What really happened?

I killed him in cold blood. He was a friend turned enemy. He knew something about my big brother that would send him and possibly my father down for life. In case you aren't aware, there is a death penalty in the state of Texas. I got my gun and I hunted him down. Tell you the truth, I think he half expected it.

Why am I with you?

Because you don't care either. Because you like a good secret. Because my gorgeous cock's got you all stupid.

No, I see him there just fallen, blood oozing, then pumping out, his face falling in realization, and he's dead. You had this gun, this intention. It's there between us now like a bond or a pact or something. What is the difference between love and ownership? And once I know the whole story on you, will I die? Friend turned enemy. It's so fragile.

It isn't like that, Mira. I love you. Just stop that and go back to sleep.

She lay in the thin electric light from the clamp-on reading lamp and watched a flea gather in and hop and gather in until it came too close to her, and she snapped it in two and smeared it along the carpet. She vowed to buy a collar for the cat at the next possible opportunity. She was just dropping back off to sleep when a series of seemingly profound images reeled out in her mind.

I see an old man, she said quietly. He's coughing and holding his chest. He gasps for a last breath that even now won't be drawn. The coffee cup he holds tilts to one side, spilling the last sip onto a pristine white bedsheet. I see an old woman running in; she shakes the man, she groans in anguish — her truly other half is dead. She is unwrapping him from the bedclothes, undressing him. She loved him. He is naked; his thin body is relaxed in death, the hair downy silver on his chest; she pets him and whispers to him. I see the old woman scrubbing the bedsheet, a froth of detergent forms as she moves the brush in small circular patterns. A tiny, almost inconsequential, yet stubborn stain holds her attention.

Sam was asleep, oblivious.

Blue Skinned Potatoes

I'm an islander, been an islander my whole life. My husband, when he was alive, fished fish. When there weren't any more fish, he fished lobster. Now, I grow potatoes using seaweed for mulch. The potatoes are called blue but they are more purple, really. Every spring I section up the little eyes and I bury them in my garden, and every fall I pull up so many potatoes I feel a certain glory at nature. I try and sell them on the mainland. The islanders won't touch them. It's a great pity. The potatoes do taste fine. Better than what you'd buy in the grocery store.

I got into farming after I lost my husband. I have a big garden. I find the work calms me. And it keeps my mind off the tragedy that lost me both Earl and my son Jake. Jake was only ten. Sometimes I think I was barely getting to know him, he was so young. Earl I never knew, I know that now.

Sometimes people from away come over on the ferryboat. I always put a little sign out that says, Blue Skinned Potatoes, and sometimes people come and buy five or ten pounds. I tell them these potatoes are related to Irish bluenose potatoes. Some people like that sort of information. It makes them feel they're eating something special, I guess.

I do like to grow root vegetables. I grew some even before Earl and that. Except for the potato bugs and a few worms, root vegetables are pretty easy growing. I like the looks of potatoes, too. Sometimes they come out of the ground looking like little round people. And I love to eat them. We used to bake them for dinner. Just a potato with butter and salt will hold a body till suppertime. Or, sliced thin and tossed with a little oil and salt and pepper and baked up in a real hot oven, there's nothing better with boiled lobster. My garden earns me a little money, enough to get by, just. I was thinking I might put a little recipe book together. Potato recipes. That might sell.

After I get my work done in the afternoons, I usually go for a walk over to the other side of the island. It's not far if I walk cross-country. I pass the school at the time when the children get out. There aren't more than about ten in that school, but I like to see them. I like to see their fresh faces and the way they run out into the playground. There's a plaque in the playground with Jake's name on, you know, a memorial? It makes me kind of happy and sad at the same time. He won't ever be running around in there. Some of the older kids do stare at me. They stare right into me. It is upsetting to be stared at. I must be upsetting to them, too. They knew Jake probably better than I did; they grew up alongside him.

I want to say to them that I tried my best to keep him here alive. I tried to hold his little gaping body together, and I could feel him struggling against dying. He really did not want to leave his friends. There was too much blood outside him and not enough inside anymore. He couldn't do anything about that and neither could I. I wish I could explain that to them, but you just can't tell things like that to little kids. I wave to them and smile but I have to keep walking. If I stand there too long the schoolteacher comes out and moves me along.

On the other side of the island is a long strand of beach. A bench was put there long ago, and that is where I like to sit. I sit for many hours some afternoons, watching the tides and enjoying the rushing noise of the ocean. I used to stand in the ocean no matter how cold it was and cry into the salt water for hours. The hermit crabs would come bite me. I didn't care. The outside of me was standing there crying, but the inside of me was still standing stiff and screaming like on the night it happened, screaming no and why and it can't be true. My clothes were soaked through with blood and little bits of flesh. I stayed shocked like that for a good year. The shock doesn't leave you too quick, I suppose.

If people saw me there on the beach they wouldn't even come down, they'd turn and go home. They used to sometimes tell Mr. Wagner at the general store, and he'd send his wife over. She'd put a blanket around me and walk me over to the bench and sit there with me if she had the time. It was kindly of her. She'd tell me about antiques she'd collected — an old pump organ, a huge old nautical painting. She's got a museum up and going now in an old shed beside the general store. Just a mishmash of old things people brought over here long ago. Earl gave her an old lead fish hook before he died. Maybe that's his one legacy. Especially now the fish are gone.

Mrs. Wagner leaves me alone on the beach now that I stay out of the water. She doesn't say much to me anymore at all. I don't get a lot of conversation here on the island. Of course, there's a lot of speculation after a tragedy like mine. It is difficult for things to get back to normal. I remind everyone about something terrible in themselves. Even though it wasn't me or my fault, it was Earl, I am guilty by association. I am, too. I accept that guilt. I don't ask forgiveness, either. I don't want it.

I take the new road, the long way home, over to the old road, just a trail really, and pass by Earl's daddy's shack up by Long Reef. Earl's daddy's a bit peculiar. I like him. He's got the only cow on the island. She's a Guernsey-Jersey mix, and she has a fine way about her. Earl's daddy looks like Earl did, only older. He's kind of on the small side, high friendly cheekbones with a fisherman's glow to them, and a head of silver hair. Earl's daddy wears a dirty jean coat that comes down past his butt and rubber boots and that's all. He won't get dressed for no one.

Hi, he says.

Hi.

After Earl did that to Jake and himself, Earl's daddy stayed home. He didn't come to the funeral nor talk to reporters, though they tried. They camped outside his shack and waited, like gulls

for the entrails, some said. After everything quieted down I had
to go find him out. I felt that was proper at least. I found him
milking the cow in the little shed he and Earl changed into a
stable. He looked up at me like I was a ghost, and then he looked
down at the teats and finished up his work. He was probably
thinking about what he ought to say to me.

You'll have to take some milk for yourself. I got too much. And
you by yourself. I can give you cheese, too. I can't eat it all nor
sell any of it. Because it's raw milk, you see.

That's good of you, I said. How you keeping?

Not bad.

He eased himself up and faced me. He picked up the bucket
of milk.

Well, he said, come inside the house. I'll make you a cup of
tea then.

Yes, that would be nice.

I walked behind him back to the house. I was looking at his
legs. There wasn't an ounce of meat on them. Gosh, that man
was skinny. Worse than Earl was. The milk sloshed out of the
bucket onto him but he didn't care or notice. Milky dew rested
on his leg hairs and then ran down into his boots. He lost a good
cup or two down into the ground, too.

It sure is a relief, he said, not to have them news people
hovering around outside no more.

I know, I know.

We didn't say anything for a long time after that. Earl's daddy
got his milk settled away in his cold cellar. He got his wood stove
going so he could boil up water for tea. That took some time.
Then he just put a tea bag in the pot of water. He used a ladle to
serve it out. I guess he didn't have much use for a kettle.

I blame the government, he said. I knew he was talking about
Earl and what he did.

Why's that?

I just do, is all. They stuck their nose into the fishery. How's
a fisherman supposed to hold his head up and feed his family
when there ain't no more fish? Now I hear there's only another

generation left of lobster fishing. The whole fishery is going to dry up. I ain't the first to say it, you know. Yes, I do blame them.

I said, Killing your son doesn't solve it.

No. I don't know why he done that.

Everyone says he was perfectly normal. As normal as you and I.

I ain't so normal, he said.

There's nothing normal about me anymore, neither.

I took a jar of milk when I left and a slab of his cheese. At home I sliced the potatoes a quarter-inch thick and left the peel on. Then I covered them with Earl's daddy's milk and cheese and baked them scalloped. I ate that over two days. I don't need a lot of food to keep me going.

I go back regularly to Earl's daddy's place whenever I need company. He doesn't stare or think too much about solving the tragedy. He said to me one time, I'm sorry for what Earl did. I doubt he did it to you, if you know what I mean. And then he stood there and shook his head.

I, too, am perplexed by what happened. When I see my face in the mirror, it has a look of worry to it. It is the face of someone who is used to being examined. My skin has been bored by the eyes and minds of many previous friends. Nobody dares ask any interfering questions. They just wonder and stare.

Like the fish hook he gave Mrs. Wagner, I'm Earl's living legacy. I am the reminder of his rampage and the letter he did not leave behind explaining his actions. I am his mystery. I am his mystery that even I cannot solve. All the people on this island know I have gone mad. They see me come home in the evening, and they look away in horror.

On particularly bad days, I go to the forest far up at the top of the island. I have a special earthen cave there where I like to curl up. I found it and dug it out further with my hands on the day of the funeral. It was going to be my own grave, into which I would fall after dying of a broken heart, but hearts are traitors of the worst kind. Mine refused to die. Sometimes I fall asleep out there in my cave in the woods. The space just hugs my body, and I am filthy when I crawl out. It is soothing, though, to be a part of the earth, and warmed. There is a whole society of small creatures underground. Sometimes I lose track of time, but no one ever comes looking for me.

Earl was dead by the time I got to him. He shot himself in the head. They said he was drunk, which is possible. He didn't drink as a rule, so he might have done it to shore himself up for what he planned to do. Jake's body was torn up with wounds. There were five. He was twitching, trying to hold on. I kept kissing him and saying, It's okay, it's okay, but he was shaking his head.

He said, No, Mummy, it's not okay.

I couldn't hold all those wounds shut. I tried. I couldn't. I had to wash all my clothes later. It was a great sadness, to wash Jake away like that.

Now, what I do is I hold onto that. I try to keep just that one wound shut. I don't want the sorrow to escape. It's my lifeblood, now. It keeps me just fine in this world, you know. I take those cold cellar potatoes of mine each spring, and I cut each little eye out and I thank it in advance, and then I bury it in my hand-tilled garden.

Falling Out

James looked in through the nursery window at the newborns. Several of the babies had escaped their swaddling and were grabbing at the air. The nurses couldn't attend them all, so some of them were squeaking, some howling. One of the babies, a scrunched up little dark-haired thing, kept being startled out of its own sleep as its reflexes spasmed. Its fingers grabbed the sky, trying to find something to latch onto. A primordial branch? Cave mother's hair? From where was it falling? From a broken bough, from grace, from heaven? To where was it falling? Asleep?

It's clutching at straws, James thought. And he ran his fingers through his lank hair and said aloud, Just like the rest of us.

It was January 27, 1986, the eve of the launch of the space shuttle *Challenger*. NASA was sending a schoolteacher up in space. Hundreds of thousands of little schoolchildren were linked by computer. Educational experiments would be conducted. James had an absurd image of astronauts in enormous white costumes, spherical glass helmets leashed by umbilical-like hoses to a red and white Tintin rocket ship. While the nostalgic pang lasted, he was an excited boy again.

What do you want to be when you grow up?

I want to be an astronaut.

We all want to rise above. That's what his father had said.

The memory compressed into a black noise in his head, a whirring. All he wanted now at thirty-eight was to rise above. Rise above despair, which seeped under his skin most days, waiting. The whirr increased, and he realized it was an external sound. He turned toward it.

A stainless steel floor polisher had overwhelmed its driver, dragging him, swaying, along the corridor. The polisher moved randomly to and fro, directed by some inner mechanism, and slammed into the walls repeatedly before changing routes. The black janitor wanly raised a thumb to James as if to say, This is cool. This is the way it is supposed to be. The polisher reached the end of the corridor and bounced like a pinball in a jammed machine, swinging the janitor wildly. Then it hovered briefly in one spot. The janitor beamed at James.

Congratulations, he said.

What?

Boy or girl?

What?

Your baby.

No, said James, I'm just looking. He felt like a thief in a department store, caught out. Just browsing, officer. Like a molester. Do you have a logical reason for being here, sir? Yes, child flesh, baby milk whiff, soft layettes, plaintive little cries. Should he feel guilty? He felt depressed. He could hear the whirr fading down the north corridor. The janitor was gone.

At admissions the secretary had asked for particulars: name, address, birthdate, health card, SIN.

Meredith looked into the nurse's eyes and said, Sin?

Social insurance number.

Oh, she said, I thought it was a theological question.

The secretary leaned over and put her hand over Meredith's hand.

She said, Are you sure about this? It isn't too late to reassess.

And Meredith said, Thank you. Thanks so much. Meredith whispered this across the cubicle as through the confessional grate. Then she smiled falsely.

The secretary's expression turned quickly from bafflement to disgust. She said, Someone will be here shortly to take you to your room, and then she turned to some paperwork.

Meredith had this effect on a lot of people, but James hadn't been put off by her acerbic nature. You're so dry, you're brittle, James had said to her when they met.

Meredith took a step back and said, Who are you?

She was young. Nineteen years old. She was a kid.

Age is no barrier, she said.

When she said it, he knew. If she could say that and mean it, then she must really have no idea, no clue whatsoever. His few friends and family asked him what he was doing. Cradle-robbing was a term that popped up.

We can bridge the gap. Look, there's an ocean of wisdom and life experience I can help her navigate.

You mean there's an ocean of depression and regret.

They had only been sleeping together for six months. He was flattered that she cared for him, even though it was obvious to him that she loved more the idea of love than anything he was able to provide. The sex was not exactly bleak, but it wasn't really working, either. It amazed him that anything could come of it. And so when she told him she was pregnant, he was elated. He hugged her. She started to cry.

I can't have this child, she said.

James said, Yes. You can.

No. It's just a dream you have.

She was right. It was his dream. He tried to shake it, but it impinged on his every thought. He bought little baby running shoes even after she'd made the appointment for the D&C. It was a dream world that still, on the eve of the abortion, brought him here to the nursery to peer through the glass at the little bundles of joy that other people would be taking home.

James felt a familiar wave of nausea fold in upon itself. He knew that this passing sensation might subside to calm waters if he was lucky, or more likely swell to a tidal wave. The nausea was shifting stomach acid right up to his epiglottis and down, curling down, cramping into his intestine. This was urgent. He needed food quickly. He fumbled as many coins as he could find into the candy vending machine behind him. He couldn't count, didn't know how much he'd put in, hoped and lucked out. He'd pressed for a Mars bar and there it was, thudding down the machine. He bent to fish it out, unwrapping it almost simultaneously, and crammed the first bite into his mouth. His system submitted immediately. He could see; he could think again.

I feel as if my body has been colonized, he had said to Meredith in describing the ailment.

You've got worms. You should get tested.

I'm not parasitic. I'm sympathetically pregnant. My body is in sync with yours.

It could be a tape worm. Or some amoebic infestation.

No, Meredith. It doesn't itch. I'm fine. It's a kind of false gestation.

Christ Almighty.

I'll bear all the pain for you.

I'm not keeping it.

James had harassed her then. He had brought her Right to Life literature, compelling arguments for a godhead in whom he himself was hard pressed to believe, and darling photographs of miniature fetal toes and fingers. And all it succeeded in doing was hardening her.

She said, I'm a kid.

He said, Age is no barrier.

She said, You thoroughly depress me.

I've bridged the gap then, he said.

What gap?

James finished up the candy bar as he walked down the corridor, simultaneously grappling with the pack of smokes tucked into the inner pocket of his frayed tweed coat. He tried to release one cigarette without taking out the packet. His heart was anxiously pumping up into his throat. He needed a smoke to thin the blood and calm his nerves. The emergency doors opened automatically.

Like the supermarket, James thought. It was an unnecessary

synaptic connection, so that in the future, whenever he went to the supermarket, this whole other flood of memories would inundate him, and he would feel sad. First his thoughts would revisit this cigarette, and then he would recall the janitor who would soon join him and who would relentlessly natter about the space program, oblivious to James's silence. And then James would remember Meredith and wonder whether she still wished him ill, which, in turn, brought him back to his rented room east of downtown in the ratty section of the city where the moment of conception had transpired, and really how pathetic that love-making had been, more sex than love, and more than either, simply an unconscious willingness on his part to father something. All of which gave him an unutterable feeling of loss. His first wife had been barren, and Meredith was the only girl since for whom his sperm had had enough gumption. And she, in protecting her own future, had denied him that little luck that he felt might have altered the rather dismal line his life had so far taken.

It was a Christer of a day. Forty-five below plus wind chill. The freezing air set his eyes into a shocked expression. The skin around his nostrils contracted painfully. The automatic doors opened again and sent up whorls of snow that smacked James along the side of his face. Snow accumulated in his ear and knocked the ember from his cigarette. It was the janitor.

Sorry, eh? Can I bum a smoke? A light? Thanks. Would you like to smoke it for me, man? The janitor laughed enough for the two of them.

James grinned but said nothing, stood there for the duration of the janitor's soliloquy, nodding and grinning as if he were half baked, a tactic he had mastered in his youth to keep most any sort of trouble at bay. The janitor started in almost immediately with a theory concerning the approaching space shuttle lift-off and his belief that its true mission was to land and populate the red planet Mars.

The fact is they're experimenting on us all the time. The fact is the climate on Mars is similar to a northern winter. There may be people living on Mars as we speak. I like to think there are Martians living here among us. The government must have a hand in all this. They must.

James was praying. He prayed as fervently and irrationally as only a non-believer can pray, and to God, not to one of the arch-angels or saints who might have less on their plates, more time to come to his aid. The prayer followed the regular pattern, Father forgive me for I have sinned, but then regressed to a sobbing inner plea for forgiveness, along the lines of strike me dead if I lie, and I swear I'll never cross you again, please please please. He carefully purged his prayer of any cursing or vanity or false idolatry. It was just, please God stop Meredith before it's too late. His inner palms, the ones he visualized right in the middle of his brain, were clasped so tight he had a pulsing headache. The janitor did not notice that James was distracted. His voice hummed in the background.

I had a cousin once, he said, lost now. Haven't seen him in eons. We used to build these pop-bottle rockets shoved full of fire cracker explosives, and we'd take them out to the field behind the old farmhouse where he lived, and we'd get far enough away so as not to come to any trouble from the grown-ups, and we'd light the fuse with matches stolen from the little variety store in town, where the lady owner tippled gin and barely noticed us chasing in and out around the candy counter and stealing whatever we could get our grubby hands on. She loved carnations, I remember, and always wore one. Crazy old lady. Anyway, striking a stolen match was a beautiful thing, my God, and the rockets would build pressure and then shoot up into a brilliant explosion. Phew! Glass splinters raining down on us, and the echoing noise, and then the stillness after that was almost religious. We were going to be astronauts when we grew up. It was our destiny. Who knows where that cousin is now? Nobody's seen him in light years. Mars maybe? Haha. Mars.

James struck a match to his cigarette. He would smoke three, and then he would go back up to her and see her sleeping and resist the temptation to kiss her as one would a child but would just look at her and recall her lying just so in his bed, beneath his tufted wool coverlet, newly pregnant and half smiling in her sleep. After the sex she had undressed him, an exposure he felt uncomfortable with, and she had found every scar from his babyhood trauma, and had drawn lines with the tip of her finger from one to the next as if these connections might give reason or possibility to that which they contained. She lingered at the extremities, his hands and feet, where the nasty scar tissue, white with age, lay like dormant stigmata. That was the last poetic moment they had shared, and the intimacy of it had terrified him.

The cigarette smoke came in like a new thought, lingered, and left.

There are two columns into which I could divide the events of my life, James thought. There is the fear column and there's the acquiescence column. Let's see — fear of loneliness, fear of fear, fear of my own edgy violence. And acquiescence. Acquiescence to my divorce, to this approaching abortion, to that same edgy violence.

James realized that there was a third column, one he might entitle fear of acquiescence, featuring a list of events which drove him to brief, mean-spirited bouts of spontaneity — running red lights, drinking himself blind, sex with intent to impregnate, then begging Meredith to let him adopt the baby. He'd done that, too. But she'd only squinted at him queerly and shook her head sadly. He first wanted to hit her or kill her or kill himself. Then he wanted to be elsewhere, hiding away in the hole that was at that minute darkening and expanding in his chest.

The janitor droned, On Sunday July 20, 1969, when the Apollo II mission returned to earth from the cratered surface of the moon, they left behind as sure symbols of mankind's conquest, a gold olive branch, a little coin engraved with the sentiments of peace from seventy-three world leaders, a variety of garbage including the clear plastic colostomy sacks that Armstrong and Aldrin had pissed into, and a US flag that blew over at take-off.

James kept smiling and nodding at the janitor, handing him

smoke after smoke, not noticing that the wind chill was chafing his neck skin and that snow was accumulating in his moustache and beard until the janitor said, Goddam cold. Then James surfaced and said, Yep, flicked his cigarette butt into a snow mound and disappeared back into the hospital.

II

Meredith wasn't allowed to eat or drink anything before the operation. She wondered vaguely, hopefully, if the fetus might not starve to death before the abortion. Her stomach was contracting out of hunger, and it felt as if a small hand was scratching delicately at her womb. She knew this was foolish. She knew it was foolish to will the thing dead. She would have to go the distance, stiffly and disconnectedly, and act as if it was all happening offstage.

A priest kept popping his head into the room, asking if anyone wanted to talk. The girl in the next bed had a few muffled conferences with him. She was frantic, distraught. Meredith understood from watching the girl and her boyfriend that it was really the boy who was desperate to have the situation cleaned up and that the girl actually wanted to have the baby. Meredith wondered if this wouldn't be a good time to ask them if they liked to swing. The girl could have James and his agenda and baggage and nurture crap, and she could get the immature freaked-out boyfriend. At least then she'd get some support.

Meredith tried to go over in her mind the events leading up to the pregnancy. But the facts kept shifting until all she was left with was the single event of the sex in James's bed the night she conceived. The bed had a tattered wool coverlet on it. It was a crazy quilt made from salvaged wool suits and winter coats. It was a cast-off from James's marriage, too. He hadn't told her this, but Meredith knew. In fact, he hadn't told her much about himself. She knew he was divorced, that his ex-wife was infertile, that they were amicable, but that was about it.

James was so ineffectual a lover even by her inexperienced standards that she couldn't believe he could impregnate her. Often he was completely impotent. He would drink himself to sleep and then wake up in the middle of the night to cuddle her. He would get up and sit at his desk in the wee hours and drink while writing poetry that he did not let her read. Hatefully, she wondered now if it rhymed. Since the pregnancy she saw their relationship as ludicrous and pathetic, evaluations she doubly gave herself since she'd entered into the affair so wholeheartedly.

As she drew lines along his scarred chest that night, she felt the poisoned beast of her imagination grow into this child in her womb. She lingered at his extremities, where the scar tissue bundled in ugly masses. She pinned him down and drew lines back and forth along him until she had emotionally flayed him. She could see his terror.

James?

Yeah?

I told you not to come in me.

Did I do that?

It wasn't exactly rape, she said.

I might have been sloppy.

A team of medical students queued alongside her stainless steel hospital bed and asked her the same series of questions regarding contraception and family planning over and over again. Some of these students were unable to hide the residue of a shriek from their voices and could not look her in the eye. Even though they could certainly overhear her answers, she enjoyed the game and contradicted herself several times.

Thank you, said the last student, a redhead with an earnest smile.

You're welcome, said Meredith. Can I say something?

Of course.

You know the doctors say if you've been on the pill for a

length of time, you should give your body a rest, that you should rest?

Yes, that's right.

Never rest, said Meredith, that's my advice to you. Be vigilant and never ever rest.

A nurse bustled in past the student and closed the curtain on her. Meredith smiled and sank wearily onto the pillow. The nurse had enormous breasts and a great card-table butt, the two separated with a pink uniform belt that cinched a waist into her figure. She had a pragmatic fussiness about her, a blotchy milk-fed round face, and an air of duty relentlessly performed. She laid a small metal tray gently on Meredith's meal cart. She plunged a thermometer into Meredith's mouth and smoothed back her hair. She whispered something unintelligible but soothing nonetheless. She turned down the bedding, turned up Meredith's nightdress. She gently removed Meredith's underpants, shimmying them down her legs and over her feet. She folded them and put them on the end of the bed. She bent Meredith's legs at the knees for her and splayed them open.

Like this, she said.

She took out an oversized cotton swab, dipped it in green antiseptic, and began to paint Meredith's genitalia. She painted Meredith's labia, her vulva, around her anus, and then swooping green stripes along her groin.

You are doing great, yes, great. You are fine. I'm sorry about this, she said. The nurse tucked her back in, took her pulse, opened the curtain and left.

Meredith turned on the television, and there was the Sally Field-like mug of Christa McAuliffe again, that damn schoolteacher. Schoolteacher-cum-astronaut.

America is a wonderful place where anyone can grow up to be the president, said Meredith. Anyone can aspire to greatness. Anyone can aspire to fly out of the earth's gravitational pull.

The girl beside her said, Oh God, the earth's gravity.

Meredith said, Christa grew up in a log cabin.

Really?

No.

The launch pad was covered in thick icicles. The sky was clear blue, the blue of a sub-zero climate. The shuttle cut its shape out of the sky. Christa McAuliffe's talking head was superimposed on the image. She was excited. She was exuberant. She was effusively happy or perhaps intensely nervous. The images were all separate from one another. That was the feeling Meredith got from the television. She saw a disconnection between the spacecraft and the sky, the astronaut and the spacecraft, and then the astronaut and the sky.

I'm wondering about the schoolteacher. Where, for her, does the separation between self and vehicle, self and sky begin?

You should talk to the priest.

A priest sees no separation. In the operating room the anesthetist will ask you to count backwards from a hundred.

What does that have to do with anything?

There is no connection.

There must be.

There isn't, that's for sure.

Meredith picked up the remote and turned the TV off, cut the schoolteacher off mid-sentence. A hush fell over the room.

The evening pall, said Meredith.

The girl beside her cried, Nurse, nurse.

A green-clad nurse pulled the curtain around the girl's bed. Meredith heard the muffled sounds of the nurse giving the girl a pill to help her sleep, then the muffled sound of the girl sobbing into her pillow.

It's okay, thought Meredith. It's fine. Tears are fine. Murders, suicides, rape, incest, bad things, bloodshed, everything.

The nurse came around with a pill in a little paper cup and a glass of water. She waited for Meredith to take it. So Meredith took it as soon as she realized this. Only she caught it in her cheek and held it there. She looked out the window at the far side of the room and waited until the last diffusion of orange light sank below the horizon, and then she swallowed the pill. She visualized the pill sliding down her throat as the sun dropping below the horizon. Sleep folded over her like a curtain.

James made his way back through the building like an automaton and came and stood over Meredith's body and marvelled at her Circean loveliness. He wondered how affected her looks were by pregnancy. He knew women who glowed when they were expecting. He curbed the desire to nuzzle and kiss her as one might a child. He half wanted to pound on her and scream at her to wake up. She had a dead look about her, that dead look that draws all the corpse's innocence into the face. She had no wariness. She might really be dead for all he knew.

He murmured, Good night, Meredith.

He backed up to a thinly upholstered leather and chrome chair, which must have been chosen to initiate in the sitter a posture of immediate concern. It was not designed for long-term sitting and certainly not for sleep. He clutched the underside, locked himself into a rigid form and shut his eyes. He woke up shrieking.

I was DOA. I died. I died. I was fucking dead.

The nurse shook him, looming into him with her wide, upset eyes, and whispered, Shh.

Meredith opened her eyes and saw him as she preferred to see him, as a blur.

James sank back into the chair and murmured, In my dream, I was dead.

She said, Would that it were.

Was is the operative, Meredith. Don't be a bitch. I used the past tense.

Meredith said, James, my cunt is green now.

What? Why?

It's cleaner that way. Less germy.

A whirring that had moments before been a faraway buzz built in intensity until it overtook the conversation. Meredith and James watched as janitor and floor polisher careened down the corridor.

Meredith said, Yellow walls the colour of sick, cleaning, cleaning, never cleaned.

Who are you talking about?

Go away, James.

I wish I could.

That teacher is going out of the earth's gravitational pull today. Will you just turn on the television?

The reporter, superimposed over an image of the launch pad and the shuttle, wore a thin business suit even though the launch pad was frozen over. He reported that, ice notwithstanding, lift-off would be in approximately two hours. All systems were go. NASA planned to overcome the ice, the cold; all problems were surmountable. Count-down in two hours' time.

The enormous nurse bustled into the room and turned the television off. She yanked the curtain around the bed, separating James and Meredith.

Excuse me, she said.

Hey, James protested.

The nurse plunged a thermometer into Meredith's mouth.

She said, You fine today? Good. They'll come for you any minute.

James stared at the curtain. He wanted to pull it open, say something useful, talk to Meredith one last time, try to be a more meaningful partner, act supportive. The curtain was drawn shut as if the play were over and the audience had missed the point. What was the theme? At what point did the resolution occur? James was perplexed. It wasn't an unfamiliar sensation. It accumulated in his intestine, cramping him. Waves of nausea broke in his stomach like a tide slapping. He started to cry quietly.

When the nurse pulled open the curtain, he was gone.

III

James ordered a hamburger with the works, a large fries, 7Up. He doused the fries with vinegar, salt and so much ketchup that his bowl looked as if it was brimful of the condiment. He looked around for a private, quiet spot to sit with his tray of food. Even though the cafeteria was mostly empty, people were scattered about singly in a way that seemed to fill the space.

Eating alone is the ultimate desolation, James thought, which did not deter him from seeking privacy. Better to eat alone, like a wild beast hoarding a meal, than to break bread with a stranger demanding conversation. He had nothing to say anyway.

A chair in the back corner looked promising, and he began the navigation through the maze of tables and chairs and people. He maintained a strained aloofness, as if to say at once, I am not here, and, You are all unimportant to me.

Hey! Hey!

James' eyes darted toward the call before his mind had a chance to stop them. The janitor was standing, waving, while catching his table to keep it from tipping over in the excitement.

You! Hey! Here. Come here. Plenty of room. What a coincidence!

James smiled broadly and switched directions. Many of the sitting customers looked up at him now as he passed, and they smiled. Some said hello. James realized that most wore hospital greens and still had masks tied around their necks: doctors and interns and nurses on their morning breaks. They looked crumpled and tired out. The janitor was grinning and nodding at James now, waiting, his head bobbing joyously.

Lift-off in an hour and a half, he said, even before James was fully seated.

James said, Yes, I heard.

Do you see it? See? The janitor was drawing his hands maniacally back and forth around his food tray. See what I've done?

No, said James.

Look. There's the cereal, bran flakes, rehydrated. The janitor was gesticulating madly. Madly. This here's the freeze-dried fruitcake. This is Lifesavers, natural form, rum butter flavour. And here's instant breakfast chocolate. It's a space meal. The janitor glared at James. I mail-ordered NASA food, he added.

Oh, said James.

The janitor plunged into the food. They got everything up there. Shrimp cocktail, broccoli au gratin, pudding, beef jerky. It's all thermostabilized or irradiated or freeze dried or rehydratable. I bought boxes of space food. I'm going to eat like this the whole time they're up there. It's my link. I got boxes of the shit. Here, have a Lifesaver.

Thank you, said James. He put the Lifesaver at the edge of his tray, picked up his fork and began eating his fries, bland, crispy wedges of deep-fried frozen potato best considered a vehicle for the ketchup. He chewed slowly.

The janitor said, That damn schoolteacher. I'm jealous as hell. I wonder if they're ever going to send a janitor up into outer space. I'd die to be the first Martian janitor, er, space management custodian. They got these Gemini sacks for feces, they got internal spacesuit sacks for pissing into, they got closed sanitation systems. They use wet wipes. They got waste management systems that recycle piss into potable water. Somebody's got to wipe down the kitchen, polish the walls and ceiling. Imagine a weightless polisher? Oh my God. Where do I apply?

The janitor was packing up his refuse, laughing. He stood up, pushing his chair away with the backs of his knees.

I best be on my way, he said. I need to get myself to a television set for countdown.

Good luck, said James. He took a bite of his hamburger and smiled at the janitor, mouth full. He lifted his hand and waved slowly as the janitor turned and rushed out of the cafeteria.

He's so happy, thought James. So damned pleased about it all.

He finished up his meal, carefully organized all the garbage on the tray and emptied it into the trash bin. He laid the tray on top of the bin. He wondered, Where is Meredith? Is she now under anesthetic? Have they opened her legs? Have they sucked out the little life? The little possibility? She must be in an operating room somewhere in the hospital. He didn't know where exactly. A masked doctor would enter her body with a small vacuum cleaner.

James knew about death. He'd been dead. He kept the laminated death certificate in his wallet as a testament to his immortality. It happened when he was an infant. His parents had left him in the crib sleeping. He had wakened, bewildered, and cried, screamed for his mother. But she hadn't come. So he had simply climbed out. He hadn't been able to do this even the day before, but he did it. He toddled out of the bedroom and opened the front door. It was a freezing cold night. Snow sparkled in a way that enticed him. The moonshine danced on the snow-laden trees, and he laughed and tried to cradle his elusive shadow in the crooks of his elbows. The cold started to freeze his feet, and he dropped down to crawl. Something sharp bit into him. There were nails, and they cut his skin, along his feet and his hands and like a roadmap on his torso. This hurt, but the cold took the edge away. He felt sleepy and succumbed to that.

His mother had found him after following the drips of blood in the snow, blood streaked snow it was in places. She swaddled him like the baby Jesus, she would relate later, and thrust his lifeless body into the warm gas oven. The ambulance paramedic took him out of the oven, unswaddled him, and performed artificial respiration. James made it to the hospital, but when they got him to intensive care he flat-lined long enough for the administration to fill in the forms. But then a young nurse had pounded on his dead little chest and screamed, Live, live. And miraculously he had done just that.

He felt that had been his moment of glory. There was no possible second act after that. Everything paled. He used to tell people that they'd have problems, too, if they'd been dead on arrival. Mostly people didn't understand that. But it was true. Death was a hard act to follow.

James wandered aimlessly through the hospital corridors

until he ended up back at Meredith's room. He switched on the television. Lift-off was in sixty seconds. The reporter's voice was shrill and excited, the camera angle was a long shot of the *Challenger*, engines roaring, to give a good view of the shuttle shooting into space. James could see that the launch pad was completely frozen over, with masses of ice build-up. The cold was brutal. It was 11:38 a.m. The shuttle left its earthly bounds and leapt into the heavens, a trail of exhaust curling organically behind it like an umbilicus or a fluffy intestine. A minute later a white cloud of liquid oxygen billowed out of the spacecraft like smoke, followed by an explosion of such magnitude that the ship shattered, the pieces plummeted. For two and a half minutes the crew cabin fell to earth, until the ship hit the surface of the ocean at two hundred miles per hour. Then silence. James caught himself swaying from side to side. It took him another half hour to process the information, by which time he had seen the explosion replayed at least fifteen times.

Meredith lay still on a gurney in a huge room, a bustling ward of post-op patients moaning back onto the terrestrial plane. Two nurses hovered, speaking to each other over Meredith.

Did you see the explosion?

What? I've been on shift. Something happened?

The shuttle exploded. Dead, all of them.

Jeez.

A wailing moan rose from one of the patients. The nurses moved away from Meredith. A man was thrashing in a sort of convulsion. The women were restraining him and calling for help. Meredith closed her eyes and turned away.

A profound feeling of trauma, of culpability seeped under her skin. A capsule of time had gone missing. And yet she had been there, neurons chemically disconnected but there nonetheless, a supine figure reminding everyone of her.

A nurse approached with a wheelchair.

You're doing okay? You're fine? I'm here to bring you back to your room.

I want to go home.

You have to wait for the doctor to discharge you.

Why?

The doctor will explain that to you.

When she got back to her room, Meredith found James asleep in the bed.

Wake up! Get the hell out of my bed! What are you doing here?

James's eyes jarred open, but his brain was still shut inside his dreams. He stuttered and slid his body out of the bed.

I fell asleep, he said. Watching the news. My eyes must have closed. I'm sorry.

The nurse helped her into bed. She curled over on her side and pressed her hand to her belly. The cramping was seismic. The nurse watched her swallow some pain medication and then left.

I feel like shit.

I'm sorry.

You said that already. I want you to pack up my bag. I want to go home.

Don't you have to wait for a doctor or something?

I'm not waiting. I'm fine. And I'm leaving now.

Meredith hobbled down the corridor to the elevator, using James as a human crutch. She took so long to exit that the elevator door would certainly have closed on her. He had never seen her looking more beautiful. Her eyes were vacuous and glazed, either residually from the anesthetic or from her cold anger toward him. He wished he could say this to her, that she was radiant. He wished he had something to say, but he didn't dare say anything at all. He just kept his finger on the open button.

Between the elevator and the hospital foyer, James saw a lump, a bag of inconsolable misery hanging by the thread of a floor polisher. The janitor's body shuddered in agony, and his blotched, weeping face looked up more or less into James's eyes.

Oh God, he said. You must be devastated.

It's all right, said James. We're all right. James realized they were talking at cross purposes, but he was too tired to care. He was propping Meredith up, holding her entire weight on his arm.

The hospital doors kept opening and closing as he shifted her weight by putting his arm around her waist.

Oh my God, repeated the janitor. I'm so sorry. I'm so very sorry. And then he half lunged, half fell forward and would have landed on James, causing a domino effect of falling bodies, himself, James and Meredith, if James had not stepped back. Instead, the janitor landed in a weeping heap at James's feet. James looked down at him and then pulled Meredith off to the side and sashayed her out through the doors.

In the truck Meredith said, I don't want to see you again.

He said, I thought not.

He drove Meredith home, tucked her into bed, and did the dishes she had left in the sink the day before. He wished she'd change her mind, not really because he wanted her to, but more because he felt it was lousy to be dumped, and unlucky, and the whole thing made him desperate. He left without saying good-bye and then on a whim bought her a bag of oranges at a local corner store. He quietly opened her apartment door, propped the oranges in front of the radiator and placed her key on top.

Meredith found the oranges later and upon peeling one, discovered that the fruit was bright red. They were blood oranges from Egypt. The sweetness of the pulp was overwhelming. She sat there and took each orange out of the bag, one by one. She carefully peeled them and broke them apart into their sections. Fifteen oranges lay sectioned on the coffee table in front of her before she started to cry.

James went home and went to work and went home in a trance-like state, which really wasn't so out of the ordinary. This was the mundane cycle of his life that, he figured, probably wasn't much different from any other life. His banal existence exhausted him and gave him a good night's sleep, all he could really hope for. And he might have been able to let this routine wash over the whole incident, purge it from his mind, if not for the recurring bouts of nausea that ranged from slight waves to belly-clutching diarrheic spasms. He had to keep food on hand at all times and contrive diplomatic ways of excusing himself at the drop of a hat so that he could rush to the bathroom. This all became so time-consuming that worry — which, frankly, had been the main impediment to action (what if it's cancer? that type of thing) — gave way to pragmatism, and James decided that first thing tomorrow morning he'd call a doctor, a specialist maybe, and provide medical history, get some blood drawn, bring in a stool sample, find out what the hell was wrong with him, anyway.

Martha's Stint with the IRA

I went into the Kmart from time to time to steal, though I'm not a bad element really. I'm Mary Martha McDonough. Everybody knows me around here. I only steal to assert my individuality and to define my sense of freedom and, naturally too, out of sheer unconditional boredom. Besides, I didn't steal the gun. I bought it. Remember that summer? The Summer of 1981. Bobby Sands starved himself to death for the Irish Republican cause, and I myself was dieting. Dieting out of respect for the moral high ground, dieting to emulate the IRA hunger strikers, shrinking for the grandness of it. I fasted on cucumber slices and mayonnaise (a per diem of 1 Tbsp), and as each Catholic dropped off, I praised myself. I was vindicated and triumphant and lovely and thin. My arms and legs felt more real to me than ever before. I walked fast to quell the hunger.

Mother said, Eat your potatoes, Mary Martha.

I can't look one in the eye.

You're not even Irish.

I'm Irish in part.

You're not. Eat. Eat.

I was Irish. I was, I felt sure. My great-grandmother was a Brady, full to the brim with the Irish blood. All that spring I read up, feasted on Ireland in the municipal library, that darkened reading room, musty and dank and voluminous, situated above the town hall; I looked down through the one tiny gothic window onto the minuscule farming village where I lived. I read every dusty tome and kept abreast of each current event, glancing down now and then to the steep pitched roofs of the little houses, their wood clad in new permanence, aluminum. I ate salted cucumber slices, one by one, out of the Tupperware I had smuggled in my satchel and read and read until everything was read, and then I walked down the asphalt main street, sidestepping cracks the ice had heaved open. I caught a ride, hitching into the city, and bought that gun, savouring the plastic imprint on my belly, the gun-shaped sweat, the sensation of reckless, false power.

The gleaming black Browning 9 mm High Power replica with its embossed grip was authentic down to the last fake clip and screw. It was easily tucked into my Wrangler blue jeans, easily pulled out again, easily aimed and fired. All lovely. But the real beauty of this heftless yet otherwise perfect made-in-Hong-Kong baby was its price. Only one dollar and forty-four cents. Truly a bargain. I kept asking myself, how could they dare, how could they? I pretended to shoot a few housewives in the parking lot, a toddler with a greener. I ran to hide behind a panelled Grand Torino wagon, and as I did so I savoured the fear, the comic realization and the relief that played out in unwinding contortions upon their faces. Oh delicate line separating seems and is, how I loved you, how giddy you made me. Laugh, I just about peed myself.

That evening I flipped to international news and thought deeply about Long Kesh and Thatcher and my poor innocent comrades. My belly crimped in glorious want, the impression of the weapon upon my skin, my hunger taking on that shape. Through the kitchen window I saw Mother, her figure corpulent and silver in the waning light, standing, stooping, a thick blur in that tangled web of garden, culling miniature cukes from the vine for pickling and monstrous, yellowed, gourdlike cucumbersomes, already bursting and spilling seed, for the composter. Cukes were brilliant. You could exfoliate with them, diet on them, moisturize with them, and if you felt libidinous, you could cut them to size. I never did that, but I did think about it. I drew the gun and popped it at Mum, widely and ridiculously missing the mark. She was a formidable target even sideways, perhaps more so sideways. I realized I would have to practice. I dove for cover just as she swung around, grabbing the telephone receiver as I did and dialling up my best friend, Paulie.

Answer. Answer. I had my free hand under my tee, you know, twisting my nipple about like a dial. The starving, the cukes and the cause, the summer heat and the gun had made me so damn horny.

Hello? His voice was gravely like a man's. He was the only boy I knew who shaved, even if only irregularly and just above the lip. We'd known each other since birth, had been, so to speak, born to each other.

Can you get the Buick?

Can't I just come over? And watch the Audrey Hepburn double feature?

No. The mum's bridge club convenes tonight.

Yeah, but what about Elwy Yost?

Paulie, come off it. I have something to show you.

We were halfway into town, Paulie steering with one hand and cramming the stub end of an Oh Henry! bar in his craw with the other. The burgundy Boat Americana, as we liked to call it, was floundering all over the highway when I unwrapped the pistol and set it on the dash above the eight-track tape deck. Paulie had Ethel Merman blaring, and he was out-bigging her, voice for voice. *You're the top! You're the Colosseum, You're the top! You're the Louvre Museum,* but when he saw the gun he stopped and gaped. His epiglottis retracted and waggled about. I could see chocolate embedded and shimmering in the grooves of his molars.

What in the bloody hell do you think you are doing, my child? he spluttered.

A dollar forty-four at the Big K.

Bleeding Jesus on the cross, and so lifelike, too.

Watch this. I waited for a stop light and targeted the woman in the car next to us. She was straining up to her rear-view mirror to apply a thicker smear of lipstick. I put the muzzle through the triangular vent window and pointed at her bleached-blond cranium. Pshew pow pow. I was into it. I made like the gun kicked back, and I smiled at her recoil, the twitch of her lip and the streak of red across her cheek where she had slipped with the cosmetic. I mouthed the words I love you as the Boat lurched and choked, sluggishly moving forward. The light was green.

Charming. That's what Paulie said. He was worried, drumming the dash with the fingers of his right hand, sitting straight up, leaning into the window, driving like an old lady. Charming, he repeated, then pressed again deeply on the gas pedal and held on through the inevitable coughing surge as the car finally recognized the command to proceed.

Car needs a tune-up, eh?

Oh shit. The grape Crush from the bottle Paulie had jammed into the ashtray followed its inertial path, sloshing up into the air in a delicate arc of purple. I had dressed with care that night. I stood naked before the mirror, and the sight of my ribs beneath my skin and, sideways, my pelvis jutting ahead of my belly pleased me. I ran my hands down my front and my fingers through my pubic hair, pulling it out horizontally. I yanked on my most torn jeans, and after many failed attempts, clothes piling like corpses on the foot carpet by my bed, I chose a green and orange striped T-shirt and yanked it on over my taupe double-A Dici Nova training bra. I twirled the gun in my fingers, snapped it back into my palm and smiled at my reflection. A sudden wave of incalculable love welled up in my chest, and I knew truly that I was ready for the Revolution.

Dinner! My mother screeched up at me. I paused on the landing to stare pointedly at the bridge foursome gathered around the Melamine card table, rolling my eyes as they made crude signals and grunted to each other, their cards curled in secrecy. Mother and Mr. Smiley, Pieter and Eva Bruin, who kept rabbits. Morris Smiley was a spindly retired newspaper man. Mother and he had a decorous relationship. She said this once to me.

Decorative, you mean.

Don't be facetious, Mary Martha.

I was pretty sure they did it. You heard things in a big old house if you listened. Long sighs and rhythmic creakings. I wasn't born yesterday. I pulled the revolver out and made as if to clean it with the hem of my shirt, though it was not dirty. I ignored, or rather pretended to ignore, the shocked expressions and the pleading eyes of the mum as I slipped the gun into my front jeans pocket. I thought of one thing and one thing only as I glared at them, focusing just above their greying heads. Tomorrow would dawn, rain or shine, regardless. The Orange Day Parade would snake its way up Main Street, past the church, Saint Catherine's Separate School, my very own, then on along by the front door of dear Father Bart's hopeless little brick presbytery, and I would be there — rain, shine, regardless. I liked the way the gun nuzzled my navel concavity at its butt, and at its tip, my pubic bone. I don't believe I had ever felt more useful or more energized than I did that day.

Mary Martha, put that thing away. When are you going to calm down? You're starving. Look at you, wasting away. For the love of God, stay home here with us and eat.

I'll not. And then I heard the rumble of Buick wheels on the gravel lane. I waved the weapon by way of goodbye, and in order to reassure Mum I said, There's nothing real about it, so don't worry. That's it, Mum, you'll worry your whole entire life away.

I looked down now at the new moist stain from nipple to navel where the cotton T-shirt had wicked in the grape Crush. It lay like a wound across my chest. The juice dribbles began to evaporate, leaving a precipitate of sugar, which felt gummy and unnatural against my skin. I scratched myself with the gun muzzle.

God I'm bored. Shall we do something?

Yeah?

Let's rob a convenience store.

Martha, really.

I bet I can. There's no reason why not.

Well, girl, last time I checked, there was some sort of law against it. Not that it'd matter to you.

Oh Paulie. Give me a real reason. Look, there's one there.

Martha!

Stop! Stop!

I slipped the Browning into my back pocket, and as the Buick rocked to a halt, I heaved the great clonking door open and, leaving it so, made for the all-night.

Paulie called after me, first, You've been advised, and then, when he saw I had no intention of listening to his advice, he yelled, Hickory Sticks and a ginger ale. Oh, and corn chips. I'll pay you back.

No need for that, lovie.

The store was over-lit. As I entered, the bepimpled cashier stashed his smutty magazine under the counter. I picked out Paulie's snacks plus a newspaper, a Mars, an Aero and a Zero bar. I went to the back to get a cold Canada Dry and a cucumber. There were no vegetables. I looked up into a convex mirror and waved, but the repulsive clerk was back at his porn. So I brought my spoils to the counter, whipped out the gun and nudged it right up his nose, the topography of which was volcanic. He was impressed. I could tell from the eyes.

You have no cucumbers, I said.

Sorry. Sorry.

Was that sarcastic?

Uh, no, he whimpered.

Okay, then, I'll let it go this time, I said. And I walked out. Simple.

In no time Paulie had the Boat and the Hickory Sticks flying, the opened pop tucked into his crotch. Viscous orange crumbs accumulated at the corners of his mouth. His unfettered gluttony irritated and depressed me. He spluttered bits and waved the bag toward me.

Have some?

No.

My stomach tightened. I'd given up my mayonnaise ration when the fifth hunger striker died. I looked great. And since Ireland was front-page news, I felt great, too. Bobby Sands,

Francis Hughes, Patsy O'Hara, Raymond McCreesh and Joe McDonnell were all dead. Martin Thurson was poorly. And the Protestants were getting out their costumes for Orange Day. It was clearly a situation of being in the right place at the right time.

Technically speaking, Paulie was saying, Hickory Sticks are not food. And by the way, how was it, anyway? You know. The robbery itself?

It was all right. Good, actually.

Eat the Aero bar. Come on, you must be starving. It's just the tiniest bit of chocolate holding the air together.

You should have seen the little creep's face. I mean, he was terrified. Glorious really.

It's not a real gun, Paulie said, and he swung across the deserted highway in a U-turn. Waves of heat licked off the burning asphalt and disappeared over the soft shoulder. The sun was vanishing. Not a red sky but instead a slowly diminishing light and an immense silence which I could not bear. It made me feel bored and sensitive, and so to gain attention I began to do shocking things with the gun. I put the muzzle in my mouth, against my temple. Then I let it hang out my open fly in a gesture of flagrant eroticism. No reaction.

Still, I wish you could have seen it, I said.

I don't go in much for that, you know.

Cicadas, like winches pulling me to them, wound their song in the still, hot night. We turned onto a gravel concession road, where a lone car barrelled past us lifting a swirl of choke-dust, which settled on the wildflowers along the soft shoulder, settled on us, too, before we got the windows up tight.

Why don't you ever come on to me, Paulie?

I do, he said. But my subtlety escapes you.

Paulie, what would you do if you had an inexhaustible sexual appetite?

Dunno, keep going?

Hypothetically, right? Your lover is spent but you aren't. You've come, say, sixteen times. What would you do?

He laughed. Sixteen times, Martha? Christ, I suppose I'd medicate.

I pressed the switch and the window hummed open. I stuck the pistol out and began to target practice. An unfortunate turkey vulture perched on a fencepost was my first victim. I watched it struggle for balance, hopping and cascading in an indignant dance until it vanished from my point of view. A farmer on a green tractor was luckier. I missed. My shot ricocheted off a telephone pole and embedded itself in the stack of hay he quietly drew homeward. I killed three sorry groundhogs and a twitching little field mouse. I took potshots at mailboxes, gleefully knocking them off their posts. I was starving. Starving.

There's an Orange Day parade in the village tomorrow, I said.

I love a parade, sang Paulie.

The cicadas began again like an air raid, and my heart, my lungs, my esophagus, my entire reproductive tract were strangely in sync with that alarming song.

Hey, listen . . .

It's the bagpipers.

No, insects.

We passed fieldstone houses perched on hillocks, one after another harbouring generations of family secrets and illnesses and passions — sexual, political, culinary, creative, violent. Hiding, too, the uncoverable stories of the mites and worms and snails and trilobites, whose traces, and sometimes the beasts themselves, were fossilized in the stone. And the purpose of this narration, piled by man or men, one rock on top of the next, was simply to give a taste of home and a shield from weather. We were retreating in time, into a spiral of hunger and whatever might come of it. There was a vortex, and I was drawn there. I could see through everything, as if the real were only a blurred web above the real real.

I'm so . . . lucid, I said.

You're Mickey Mouse! It was the high point of Ethel Merman's career, that one line, and Paulie sang it like a pro. He took hold of my hand then and squeezed, stopped the car along the ditch, half in it, really. He got out and came around and helped me out. He put his body gently against mine. The pistol pressed into me, tight into my ribs, and Paulie's phallus pressed on my jeans, too. I lost my balance, and we tumbled down the bank into the dry ditch, where amidst the primrose, vetch and clover, of which I found, afterwards, in the dark, a four-leaf, we rubbed together and plunged into a fervent and barely aborted sexual intercourse. This and the heat and the occasion spent Paulie. He ejaculated into his hand and wiped it in the grass.

Look at the clover, Paulie, I said.

Fodder.

No, luck.

Fodder.

Fuck. I yanked a fistful up and tucked it into his mouth, enough of a mass to jam his throat and set him rasping and spewing. He retched green, slumped into the ditch and fell asleep. I lay beside him until I, too, fell asleep, night and sleep descending like a movie clapboard, eyes snapping shut. And then, as if no time had passed, the night crickets gave way to the whine of a distant piper and day. I awoke, my stomach pulsing, a whinging contraction of emptiness. I rose and marched as if still in a dream along a seeding lilac hedge toward the fife and drum, away from Paulie. I made my way over fences, not electric nor barbed nor split wood, not stone heaped upon stone in an effort to clear the damn field nor wire with little pressed maple leaf decorations, not gnarled bone-like tree-root barricades, but rather the rusted, decrepit remains of a time-line of automobiles, broken, smashed, incomplete, a disassembly of rotted upholstery, groundhogs and vespiaries.

Paulie shouted after me, but I ignored him. Or tried to. The further I went from him, of course, the more his speech dwindled in volume, but in direct proportion its resonance increased. He had begun loudly in a melodic, affected Irish schoolmarm accent, with an account of the Boyne skirmish — William of Orange on his white steed rearing and trampling the papist army — and ended with a shrill declaration of my insanity.

You're out of your bleeding head, Martha.

You've got a strange way, too, Paulie, I whispered.

I stumbled toward the parade though rasp- and blackberry canes, which smeared me and scratched at me, but I pushed my way through anyhow, treading now and then into ancient pioneer dumps of rusted tins and medicine bottles, whisky salve. The bagpipers' screechings were clear now. I came into the open air and screeched along with the tune until, coming into town, I could no longer hear myself, so loud were the pipers. A fat man dressed as King William, sabred and straddling a white gelding, pranced ahead of the marchers. The paraders were decked in orange and blue sashes and royal purple hats. Some donned bowlers in the tradition of Belfast Orangemen, and all had their collars and their attitudes. Blissfully unaware, stupid in the extreme, the crowd waved at the floats and accepted candy and balloons and silly little Union Jacks from the marchers. Half of them were Catholic, the ignoramuses.

What does it do to you, Martha? Paulie had snuck up behind me.

It gets my ire up, I said.

The Browning slipped nicely into my hand. To me, the parade was a herd instinctively moving forward toward a gleeful and pointless collectivity, each face flushed and swollen in the heat. Their animation fed me. It was difficult to tell one parader from the next, but I had my target chosen. He was bringing up the rear, fumbling a sort of flag-cum-baton. I chose him because he was alone, because he was bulging out of his undersized uniform, and because I had a clear shot. I knew what he was all about; I could see right through him, entirely. And so, thinking only of my compatriots at Long Kesh prison, I took careful aim and pulled the trigger.

It was only then, as the bullet left its chamber, that I saw her. Mother was not in the parade but had somehow become caught up into it. She carried two paper bags of groceries, one in the crook of each arm. The crowd jostled her into a variety of uncomfortable positions. She tried to pause but was inevitably nudged forward. This would be a story she would want to tell later with shrill fury, how she had been menaced and abused by an infantile pack of revellers. How it badly affected her card playing. How it badly affected everything she did for the rest of her life. She was aghast, I could see, her buttery cheeks puffed yet further out, her rose-grey permanent splayed in anxiety. Then suddenly I saw her washed out pink hairdo jerk back, as if hit by some un-measurably huge force, a hole in her forehead appeared for a second, then a gush, a stream, a river, a pool of lifeblood. Something had gone terribly wrong. Trying desperately to connect the disparate, I looked down at my weapon.

It can't be, I said. For god sakes, it's only just plastic.

Paulie took the pistol, wiped it carefully on his shirt, spit on it, wiped it again, let it drop and pulled me toward him, and, even as I fainted, he said, You must be famished.

Batterie Todt

Christiaan Derycx and his wife, Maddy, took their holidays, what little they had, with their three sons in Picardy, France, without fully realizing what they were venturing into. They boarded a chartered flight from Pearson into Zaventem airport (dirt cheap, even if the cabin door stuck at take-off) and rented a brand-new slick black Mercedes, which suited Christiaan's notion of where he ought to be in his life even if he wasn't there yet, and headed out for a five-day ramble through the countryside. Christiaan wondered briefly how his new secretary, Alison, was managing without him. Maddy, Luke and Andrew had a singalong to keep Ivan from wailing his little head off in the unfamiliar rented car seat.

> *The lake, it is said, never gives up its dead,*
> *Till the skies of November turn gloo-meee . . .*

It was Maddy's idea, this holiday. She had said she thought it would be interesting to see the northern part of France where Flemish, or rather a francophonic turn on Flemish, was spoken, especially since Christiaan's family had emigrated from Flanders in the 1950s. With only a week of holidays, Christiaan felt that Maddy had somehow railroaded him into this particular travel plan. It bothered him that she hadn't consulted him, that she'd made assumptions; he didn't know why it bugged him, but it did. The Caribbean might have been nice this time of year. Christiaan's Flemish parents had come over as potato farmers when he was two and, of course, had higher aspirations for their only son. Christiaan had gone into publishing and now managed a series of glossy pharmaceutical product-placement magazines for a well-known communications conglomerate. He hadn't left much to guesswork for Alison, but there were a few accounts that he wasn't able to finalize before he left. Everything would almost certainly be okay; he'd call her tomorrow, maybe sooner.

They decided to head through Belgium to the ocean and then follow the coast, first down to Cap Gris Nez, then to Cap Blanc Nez. Christiaan pointed out the Chunnel opening to the boys just as a TGV train hurtled out of the earth. They got a good look at the English Channel, too. Luke had done a school project on the Spanish Armada — a diorama in Maddy's Pyrex lasagna dish using modelling clay for the land forms and an Armada ship formed out of beeswax. Maddy had brought binoculars.

I don't want you boys going through life thinking the Isle of Wight is a hunk of green and pink Plasticine, she said. Maddy was a freelance writer (book reviews, mostly) before the children came along and complicated things. Now she stayed at home and made (in Christiaan's opinion, though he knew to keep his mouth shut) peculiar miniature iconic paintings of postal workers, street cleaners, housewives, garbage collectors, etc. They had something to do with the heroics of just getting through the day or something. The paintings were her way of wading through the boredom of domesticity while Christiaan went to work (she'd been successful at a co-op group show on Queen West; comments like "searing" and "provocative" appeared in the gallery guest book). When he looked at the paintings, Christiaan couldn't help but wonder about that old stereotype of a bored housewife having a relationship with the postman. He thought that would just about be perfect. That would about take the cake. Maddy fixed gold leaf haloes on her postmen with Elmer's Glue.

But I can barely speak Flemish, honey.

It's the light I want to see — you know, those Netherlandish paintings from the Middle Ages. The yellow gold. The essence of godliness in the lush green grass.

I wonder what the light is like in Jamaica. Warm, I bet.

Aw, Christiaan, really. I thought you'd appreciate this. It's your roots.

Potatoes are my roots.

Christiaan fiddled with the radio in the Mercedes until he found a station that played French pop-rock; he'd heard enough renditions of "The Wreck of the Edmund Fitzgerald." The landscape shifted abruptly. Massive holes in the ground seemed too uniform in their concavity; Maddy began pointing them out to Christiaan.

There's another! What are they?

Yes, I see. They line up, I think.

And then it dawned on them both. These were bomb craters, grown over with meadow and cropland. Here and there cattle grazed. The bovine eyes looked up as Christiaan slowed the car alongside the road. First World War? Second? It wasn't that Christiaan hadn't been taught about the German presence in the north of France; he'd just associated that with Normandy. And the fact was that the history taught in school hadn't really sunk in.

Of course, Maddy said. The War.

What war? asked Andrew.

The big one, she said.

Gitche Gumee?

No, stupidy, said Luke. She means World War I, doesn't she, Dad?

I'm pretty sure these are from World War II. I think.

Christiaan recalled friends in high school who were weapon freaks, and in grade ten, he had done a project on the Holocaust — Bristol board, Magic Marker and pasted cut-outs from old magazines. He knew a great deal about Auschwitz, or was it Treblinka? Anyway, his information was pretty damned specialized. Christiaan couldn't remember ever even looking at a military map. Of course there had been the obligatory battle dates to memorize. A battle that had to do with defending England was memorable. Was it 1939 or 1941? He suddenly remembered the girl who sat in front of him — Mary Damer — and her long blond hair, her coquettish confidence. Sometimes when she swung her head, her hair would toss onto his desk and lie there.

Is that a bunker?

I think.

A farmer in a blue coverall waved when Christiaan slowed the car to look at his bunker. Beyond a cenotaph or a war museum or two, Christiaan hadn't expected to see actual evidence of war. In fact, he hadn't ever really visualized, much less internalized, what a war was. Maddy whispered to him that she could sense the dead. She pulled up the sleeve of her blouse; the hair along her forearm stood up in an alarming way.

We could turn the car around or else head to Paris, Maddy said.

Why?

I just thought. They're young, maybe.

The boys were screaming out the back windows, arguing over the electronic window opener. Then they started shooting each other — machine gun buzz. Christiaan waved and smiled to the farmer.

Gosh, the French are adorable — the little hat, did you see? he said.

Calm down back there, said Maddy. Hey, there's another one. Look, another bunker.

They're all over, Mum, pewpew-pewpewpew, got 'em, nasty Kraut.

Andrew, who taught you that?

Look! Look at that.

The land jutted out over the English Channel into a sheer cliff, hundreds of feet above the water. Christiaan found a shoulder on which to pull off the road, and he and the two older boys jumped out and trespassed across a field where wildflowers and the first real poppies they'd ever seen grew between the cow pats. Maddy kept Ivan in the car.

Life is vertiginous enough already, she said, as they headed away. They should put up fences. It isn't safe. But they couldn't hear her anymore.

Don't the cows ever fall off, Dad?

Slow down right now, buddy, Christiaan said, or I'm taking you right back to the car.

Christiaan got the boys to lie flat on their bellies and shimmy the rest of the way to the edge, until their heads hung over the cliff and they could get a good view of life's infinite possibilities. He didn't really understand what Maddy meant by vertiginous; he liked the thrill, that falling sensation he got from looking down vast depths. It made him feel, if not alive, then certainly sensual. There was something arousing in fear, wasn't there? Possibly Maddy didn't like to be aroused; there were hints that that might be the case. Or maybe she just didn't like him, although most other people did, so he found this possibility irrational. It sure was a long way down.

A thin mist rose out of nowhere, as if it was raining up instead of down. Christiaan realized that they really ought to continue if they were ever going to make it to Arras in time to find an auberge for dinner and the night. Or if they turned around, like Maddy had suggested, they could still drive back to Bruges and find an overpriced but non-confrontational hotel, spend the remaining five days as tourists, taking punts through the lock system, eating mosselen-frites and maybe getting a view of that famous Bosch triptych Maddy had harped about. He raced Andrew and Luke back to the car, making sure to let them win. He felt so un-encumbered, so free spirited away from home. Maybe Belgium was the better plan, easier, safer.

Shall we go back up to Bruges, then?

Bruges?

Hey, it's up to you.

The boys circled around their legs, sniping at each other, and even though the children were apt to break into this sort of military aggression anywhere, at any time, Christiaan knew that Maddy felt that this landscape inspired such behaviour and that it wasn't right or proper for little children to be exposed to war and other grown-up activities. He realized suddenly that this place made her extremely uncomfortable, yet not nearly as uncomfortable as explaining it all to him would be. She would probably think that Christiaan ought to sense how she felt. It was like having to explain the punchline to a joke — something was always lost in the translation. If you didn't get it, you didn't get it. Christiaan did get it, but he preferred the pretense of silence and the cruelty of letting her squirm. There was something interesting about the subtext of her confusion and something about marriage that made him want to hold her hostage. If she had something to say she should speak her mind. He wasn't going to pretend he could read it.

Why is it always up to me? Maddy finally said.

Fine, then. It might be nice to spend the afternoon in the French countryside.

But . . .

Don't worry, honey, you ride shotgun. I'll answer questions.

You think they're old enough?

Absolutely.

The magazines that Christiaan published were a hybrid of advertisement and editorial. The editorial was designed to meet a certain target group, for instance, senior citizens or teenagers, and had the sole purpose, albeit veiled, of selling consumer goods. In linking content to product, Christiaan had found a niche market for his own particular skills. He had a knack for empathy — placing an up-beat yet sensitive article about mastectomy on the same page as an expensive name-brand hair dye or a posh out-of-town spa, that sort of thing. He planned to make a killing and then spend it on the little luxuries that made life bearable — costly single-malt Scotch, a car such as this, a bigger TV with more clarity, quality name-brand toys for the boys. He had enjoyed holding the boys as he levered their little bodies over the cliff's edge. It gave him a surge of love.

Christiaan saw a bunker off the road up ahead. He riled the boys into a frenzy and marched them in straggly formation, meanwhile haranguing them to keep their chests out, their chins and knees up, etc. The boys were thrilled.

Nothing so effective as military endeavour to enliven the hearts of little boys, Christiaan said, looking back at Maddy.

Luke said, This sucks, as he pulled an invisible firearm out of a non-existent holster.

I've got you covered, you conniving minion, Christiaan said. He had his hand shaped into a pistol, the muzzle of which was at Luke's temple. Drop your weapon and keep marching, hup-two, hup-two, three, four. I could have had you court-martialled for that.

Sir. Sorry, sir. Luke saluted.

Jesus, Christiaan.

The first bunker was built into a hill above the now slightly graded cliff overlooking the English Channel. Once they got into it they realized that it was one of a series of small, cave-like hostels fabricated out of reinforced concrete and dug into the earth. One or two of them had washed-out slogans on the walls inciting hatred of Winston Churchill. The German was almost impenetrable for both of them — "The future is bleak" and maybe "You will collapse, never Germany." The exterior walls were riddled with bullets; rust washed out in rivulets down the sides. Maddy took Ivan into the bunker that seemed to offer the least risk of danger and sudden death, clutching him along his pudgy forearm and clearly against his will (he wanted to walk), while Christiaan took the older boys into the less accessible bunkers hidden along the cliff edge. The interiors were mouldy rather than creepy, and they stank of stale human urine. It was obvious to Christiaan that the local farmers used the bunkers as latrines nowadays.

He watched as Maddy carried Ivan on her hip across the switchback road and into an apparently disused meadowland. The sky was an opaque grey. Maddy wore a peasant dress, retro-haute in Toronto but dowdy here; she looked like a farmer's wife — nothing like what Christiaan thought his wife should look like. He wondered whether the choices he'd made were the right ones. He tried to imagine his life if he changed them; of course, there were always options.

The boys ran to catch up to her, and he hurried to follow, not wanting anything to happen to them on the road. The fields were straw gold and lush green, the grass growing thickly around the unscythed hay from previous years. Here and there, as far as he could see, were huge pockmarks where bombs had burst through the crust of the earth. What bodies had been eradicated? Who? Each hole held a history of disappearance, negative space. The boys ran down into the pit of a crater. Ivan peered at them from the perimeter of the five-metre hole.

You know what that is, Luke? Maddy said.

No. Yeah.

It's where a bomb exploded.

Neat. I knew that.

Yes. People likely died.

They did? In this hole?

Yes, possibly.

Neat.

Christiaan headed back to the car. By the time Maddy and the boys got there, he had already swept out the detritus that had accumulated in the short trip — raisin boxes, Kleenex, transformer men, scattered raisins, crayons, finished dot-to-dots and mazes that served no purpose once completed. Looking over the map, he had ascertained that making it to Arras was a pipe dream that he didn't really want to pursue; he was enjoying the childish rhythm the day had taken on, and if they made it as far as St. Omer, that was good enough. He wanted to leave Cap Gris Nez and drive around the countryside, just play it by ear.

We'll have to rush, Maddy said, after she'd buckled the boys in and sat down in the passenger seat. Christiaan leaned over her lap and fussed with the glove compartment. The Michelin was incorrectly folded and had jammed the door hinge.

Dammit.

Let me.

Aach.

I got it, I got it.

Maddy pulled the map out and unfolded it until it obscured the entire windshield view, took careful note of the creased edges and re-folded it into a neat rectangle. This took longer than necessary. Maddy was making the work seem complicated. Christiaan decided to ignore this, whatever it was, and look out the driver's side window along the eastern horizon. He was trying to remind himself of the obvious fact that Maddy was a good mother, when he spotted what appeared to be the outline of a gun. The boys had seen it, too.

A gun, said Andrew. A German K5 that shoots across the channel, eh, Lukie?

I'd say. Aw, cool. Can we go see?

Dad?

That can't be a real gun, boys. It's way too big. It's got to be a model, said Maddy.

No. It's a K5. Part of the Nazi Atlantikwall, uh, uh, a railway gun, yeah.

School?

Nuh, History Channel.

As they approached the massive artillery gun, they saw the enormous bunker behind it. Emblazoned in huge black letters along its curved exterior wall was its name: Batterie Todt. The concrete structure was fenced and gated, hours were posted; it was a military museum of sorts, clearly privately owned and therefore, perhaps, of dubious quality. These entrepreneurial ventures were often fly-by-night, the owners untrustworthy, case in point, the place should by all rights be open now. Maddy was for continuing on.

Luke and Andrew were adamant. They must go in. Christiaan saw so little of his boys in the normal scheme of things that he was hard pressed not to give in to their desires. Besides, he was curious. He liked the emotional effect of the bomb craters and the cliff, and now the chromatic green paint on the artillery gun. The nudging sense of danger, past danger, was almost physically stimulating.

A man emerged from a little stucco cottage next to the Batterie, hitching his trousers up and checking his fly. Christiaan
considered him somewhat unsavoury. The man said something
unintelligible in a language so far from any French or Flemish
ever encountered by either Maddy or Christiaan that the two
were obliged to nod maniacally and point.

What's he saying, Mum?

He's certainly a character.

I don't get it. What did he say, I said?

Andrew, I haven't got the foggiest idea.

It cost thirty francs to enter the museum, children free. The
foyer was an inundation of memorabilia — German medals
featuring tanks and bombs, a sampler of Chantilly lace featuring
a tatted Stuka bomber, undetonated grenades, bullets, German
and British pistols and medallions, caps, naval memorabilia,
decks of well-thumbed playing cards. It was an assault to the
eyes, impossible to take in. Maddy was drawn to the lace-work
— the craft and exhaustive effort fascinated her.

Imagine tatting a bomber, she said. A grieving widow made
that, I bet.

The owner indicated the direction of traffic flow inside the
bunker. The concrete ramp inclined downward, and on either
side, a glass wall enclosed more and varied war artifacts. One was
meant to follow the path like a lamb to the proverbial slaughter.
They were the only guests; Christiaan could hear their own
remarks dampened and absorbed into the dank walls. He thought
of the little hand grenades as he passed through the corridor and
checked his back regularly. This place made him a little nervous.

It's a Nazi bedpan.

With a Swastika.

What's a bedpan?

There's a bomb, a big one.

Mustn't touch, honey.

They peed?

Christiaan was trying to decipher a couple of foxed and
yellowed Nazi propaganda posters. The advertisements seemed

so naive to him, so obvious. One featured a skeleton hurling a bomb onto a house: "The fiend sees your light! Black out!" Another promoted a small, handsome battalion surging ahead to the front: "Infantry: The Queen of the services." This one held Christiaan's interest for a long time. It reminded him of an ad he'd recently featured in the placement magazine *Grown Up* (the title was his brain child). It was a promo for an incontinence item describing itself as thin and seamless — the queen of adult diapers. Christiaan began to ponder the word infantry. He pictured a troop of soldiers clad only in diapers. Another, more troublesome, work memory seeped in then. Christiaan saw himself in his mind's eye back in the office on the phone, trying to chat up a writer. He wanted an editorial about an upscale spiritual/yoga retreat where, for a fee, one could have a milk and rose-petal bath, and all the cares of the world would fall away. The beauty of all this was that the retreat was locked in to advertise in a future issue, and money would simply make itself. His perky new secretary, Alison, came in and stood expectantly in front of him, clutching a batch of fresh messages. Her smile cracked her lipstick around the corners of her mouth. Was she mouthing the word "Lunch"? She had on a peach-coloured skirt that clung along her panty hose to her thighs.

There was an allure to the notion that people were available to him. They might expect something from him in return, but generally only something that didn't affect him, or if it did, affected him positively, like a promotion, or the shifting over of more responsibility without giving actual credit. It was obvious from the way she acted that Alison was an empire builder. He imagined having sex with her, pushing up against the flimsy drywall on the window side of his office. He imagined the crackle of static electricity as he pulled her synthetic skirt up her legs. It would be easy to fire his coordinator and instate Alison in the position closest to him. He would let Alison make managerial decisions, let her in peripherally on the workings of the company. He might make it seem that they were a team. It would be a horny lie, cruel if he thought of it from Maddy's perspective, but he would try very hard not to do that. It only had to last until his interest in Alison waned, at which point he'd break it off. Then the lie would dissolve, ipso facto. He tried to picture what would happen if Maddy found out, but he couldn't get his brain much past the view of Alison's pantyhose lying in a heap on the mottled green wall-to-wall in his office and the look of abandon around her mouth as he socked it to her. Hmm.

Christiaan moved into a seeping underground room that had an endless series of rifles fixed to the walls. Each rifle had an old-fashioned cardboard price tag threaded around the barrel bearing, instead of a price, a date; there was an assortment of guns from the twenties, thirties and forties, from England, Germany, the USSR. There were a few modern Kalashnikovs that Luke said he thought were Pakistani imitations. Luke and Andrew became mesmerized by several mock-ups of real bunker life. The museum owner had propped up battered mannequins and dressed them in a hierarchy of uniforms, as befitted a crew. He'd pinned an iron cross on the officer. The crew members were heavily armed, even while sleeping on the canvas cots.

Look at this guy, whoa.

Christiaan wasn't sure if the boys were saying nasty or Nazi. At any rate, they took turns loading their increasingly more deadly imaginary weapons and shooting down the enemy. The mannequins' glassy expressions made it even funnier for Luke and Andrew. They looked the same, dead or alive. Maddy heaved Ivan up and tucked him into a baby back-pack strapped onto Christiaan. Ivan's eyes were already closing. Luke and Andrew found a weakly cordoned area housing a large and dubious canister, unmarked. They were breaching the wall and using the canister as shelter from each other's blasts.

Christiaan?

He looked up and over to Maddy from a central glassed-in display case. He had been staring for some minutes at a maquette of the entire Atlantikwall. Typed in English was some information: Fritz Todt, the museum's namesake, had been the engineer and later ammunitions and weapons minister largely responsible for this impenetrable strategic military wall. The German army had arrayed huge jaw-like metal traps along the beaches, dragon's teeth, to make tank landing impossible for the allied troops. Meanwhile, the gun in front of Batterie Todt wreaked havoc on the English beach. It had the power to shoot across the twenty-eight-kilometre channel onto Kentish beaches. Christiaan wasn't really able to absorb this information. He couldn't get Alison's pale, thin legs out of his head; it was like a nervous tic.

Honey?

It's getting late . . .

We'll eat in St. Omer, maybe find a hotel there, too.

It must be getting dark. How far is St. Omer?

Not too.

Luke, Andrew and Christiaan, with the baby asleep on his back, climbed the metal stairs onto the railway gun. The railroad track had been cut away after the war. Christiaan imagined that the owner of the museum and possibly his mother had reclaimed their ancestral farm soon after the line was dismantled. At first the presence of the massive bunker had probably distressed them, a daily material reminder of the miserable fate of the father, who Christiaan imagined had died in an early and embarrass-ing military retreat. The boys straddled the gun, climbing as high as Christiaan would allow (which was as high as Christiaan figured Maddy would allow). Afterwards, they dawdled back to the Mercedes. The leather upholstery already smelled like rotting apple, urine and talc. Christiaan looked over the Michelin and found the best route to St. Omer. Maddy reached into the glove compartment for a piece of dark chocolate. The sun was setting (a line of orange, then nothing), and still the fog was blurring everything.

Christiaan stopped at a bakery en route and had Maddy jump out to buy the last now-stale baguette to hold over the famished children. Ivan awoke and began wailing again; Luke and Andrew spiralled into furious argument in the back seat, pestered each other into rages and then placated one another with toilet jokes. By the time they drove into St. Omer, everyone was irritated and exhausted. It was Christiaan who found the restaurant-hotel (two and a half stars) with a children's menu. By then it was eight o'clock, and jet lag had fully set in. The salty mist had turned to an insipid, mizzling rain.

The maitre d' seated them at the back, behind a green metal screen with a tree-of-life punched into it, far from the other customers. Maddy and Christiaan investigated the menu for the one or two items the children might be likely to find appetizing. The boys were restless and whiney. Ivan pawed at them from under the table, alternately meowing and barking.

Here's something — bifteck au pierrade avec frites.

Boys, boys. Steak and fries?

Do they have ketchup?

No. Mayonnaise.

No ketchup? Why not?

They don't do ketchup in France.

Do they do peanut butter?

On fries?

What's "au pierrade"?

Maybe that's the chef's specialty. The French are quaint.

The waiter was dressed elegantly in black and white with an immaculate apron tied around his waist. He had a neatly trimmed pencil-line moustache, a fresh haircut and a bustling, nervous aloofness about him. He was a career waiter.

Oui? Qu'est ce que vous pouvez manger ce soir?

He brought a basket of fresh rolls and glasses of Orangina and milk to quell the rising tide of infantile dissent. For Maddy and Christiaan he brought a decent bottle of house red. Within minutes, he brought in the first plates. Heaps of crisp french fried potatoes formed a crescent moon along one side of each plate; a small ceramic condiment bowl held a large quantity of yellowish mayo; the flank steaks lay glimmering red and wounded — firm, glistening, raw slabs of flesh. The waiter swung about and hurried toward the kitchen as Maddy and Christiaan sniffed anxiously, their eyes widening in simultaneous horror. Did the French serve raw meat to their children? How do you say "raw" in French? "Au pierrade"? Christiaan and Maddy stared in confused disbelief at one another. The faint whiff of the slaughterhouse lingered in their nostrils. Briefly, Christiaan contemplated confiding in Maddy his imaginary transgressions with Alison. She would laugh at him. It would bind them together, draw her in to him somehow. Luke and Andrew were poking at the meat, watching the flesh indent and slowly return to form.

It's cold, Mum. Is this meat cooked?

Quiet, honey. Just eat the fries for now.

We get to eat raw meat? Cool.

Without ketchup.

It would look better with the ketchup. More bloody.

God, the French are cool.

Just eat the fries. Okay?

The mayonnaise could be an infection.

Shh.

The waiter, their salvation it turned out, came back and placed two sizzling hot rectangles of stone on the table.

Au pierrade, he announced.

Au pierrade?

Oui, c'est ça.

The children took turns flinging slices of meat at the hot stones and shrieking as the steam rose. The bilingual pamphlet Maddy picked up later said: Cook your meat on stone! The camaraderie of a campfire developed as meat was hurled and cooked and eaten slathered in mayonnaise. Christiaan kept bursting out in spontaneous laughter at the misunderstanding; the resolved anxiety gave him a release. By God, he was having fun.

That was some weird museum, Maddy said. I've never seen or imagined anything like it.

Did you see the guns for sale?

Really?

In a display case, near the exit. Two Kalashnikovs. Cheap. What would people do with such a thing?

Kill?

How do you get a licence to own an assault weapon?

Really, how would I know?

They took a double-occupancy room upstairs. Maddy read to the boys and then stayed with them until they fell asleep. The rooms were renovated in a slipshod fashion with salmon-hued wallpaper and a fleur-de-lys border. The mattresses were soft and thankfully unbowed; they had to push two singles together to make a double for themselves. The one-channel television featured a Las Vegas-style variety show. Maddy and Christiaan took turns showering in the half-size bathtub (those prepackaged mini-soaps), and slipped into bed wearing T-shirts and socks. Then Maddy started to cry and surprised Christiaan by being unable to stop easily.

What is it? he asked, not sure he wanted to know.

This is such a crazy holiday, that's all.

Stop that. The boys are having a great time.

Christiaan caught hold of her moist chin and looked deeply into her eyes.

Je t'aime, he said. It was so lovely to say it in French, so florid and easy.

Maddy grinned vaguely through her tears. Then she said it, spat it at him really. Je t'aime aussi.

She confused him. Perhaps he should have told her about Alison, but now it was too late. He couldn't make it a whimsy after the tears, the meat, the foreign I love you. He patted Maddy along her forearm and told her instead about the girl in front of him in history class, how he couldn't get her out of his head all day, her sexy hank of blond hair, trimmed to perfection, and the sway of it as it landed, erotically charged, in front of his pubescent eyes, and how the confusion of it at the time had made him fondle himself and sometimes cry late at night. Then Christiaan lay very still on the hotel bed until he was sure Maddy had fallen asleep so he could feel safe to do the same.

The Last Magic Forest

The forest was lush. Needles turned brown, cedar cones spilled seed along the floor in matted thickness. Rocks nourished pink and green lichen; mushrooms sprouted like heads on long necks in the speckled light. The floor rippled with small creatures, breathing and shifting and eating. Blueberry shrubs and thickets of cedar and black spruce grew spindly, barely worth the bother. Yet they'd cut it down. No one came in with chainsaws or double-handled saws or axes. A huge machine called a feller-buncher grabbed each tree and cut it off at the base. The little nipple of land was cleared in less than an hour. The small creatures came out when the thunderous noise quietened and looked about and sniffed the changed air. The black bears, who had retreated to the remaining forest, stood on hind legs and pawed the air and roared their discontent.

The carnage wasn't over. A bulldozer scarifier pushed all the forest debris into little corridors, leaving the thinnest layer of topsoil and shoving the rest into eight-foot swells containing roots, sand, soil, leaves, unfortunate field mice shocked to death and buried alive in the onslaught. The driver patterned the destruction into a labyrinth. The land was flanked on two sides with scraggy forest and blocked from scrutiny on the third by a slash pile some fifteen feet high. Sharon had to climb this to bag up her seedling trees. Three hundred or so fit in the three-bag affair that was harnessed to her. She had to climb back over the slash heap to reach her plot, a tit of land, as the crew boss called it.

Smells bear, she said.

Jeremy, the guy in the land next to her, wouldn't hear her or a bear roar over that slash heap. It was early spring. The bears were sleepy and hungry. The moose were horny, in rut. The landscape was infused with the stench of wet bear fur and scat. She stood still at the opening of the corridor, looked over the slash, felt the dragging weight of the water-saturated trees on her waist, the nylon belt rubbing on the skin there, and breathed. The bear odour choked her, it was that thick. A death paranoia palpitated in her chest. She would die here. The bears, though not prone or habituated, would devour her, and her screams, too, would die on the breeze. Black bear attacks were unusual. She had nothing to fear but fear itself. That was no small thing.

Sharon pulled the elastic band from the first pack of twenty-five trees and let it drop to the ground. She eased a tree out of the tangled root mass, held the bundle in her shovel hand and got to it. The shovel blade was ground down to a thin, almost dibble-like instrument. It was sharpened with a diamond stone. Her technique was simple but honed to the point of rhythmic perfection. The shovel was aimed and thrown into the ground. The standards were six feet by six feet. The blade lacerated the earth, she drew the shovel toward her, laid the root stock horizontally and shoved it into the hole with the help of the blade of the shovel and the edge of her callused hand. She withdrew the shovel blade and used the heel of her boot to close the gape of earth over the roots.

Every hundred trees she whispered, Grow fuck.

Every three hundred trees she'd bag out and head back to the tree stash for more trees and a few Oreo cookies. Sharon crapped in the corridor next to a freshly planted tree, quickly, slapping at mosquitoes and blackflies. A bug-bit vulva could spoil the day. The flesh everywhere was bundled against the flies. She had a T-shirt wrapped around her head and tied with a bandana laced with DEET. Her shirt buttoned at the collar, stank of sweat build-up, dried and again soaked, Watkins bug dope, citronella, and some Avon product that was designed as perfume but worked surprisingly well against the northern Ontario insectarium. Eight cents a tree, fifteen hundred trees a day. She wasn't a lifer. It paid the university tuition.

The grass that had eked out an ecosystem was already long, some blueberry shrubs that had survived the scarifier were growing askew out of the slash pile. In the morning the residual bear reek was profound, inescapable. There was evidence. Not only droppings but also damp, flattened grass where the bears had slept. She could see, in her mind, the shadowy creatures lumbering off when they sensed her approach each morning. They hid, camouflaged by the forest, around the plot, sniffing her like cartoon bears, roughly and larger than life. They held her in a position of esteem. They held her in ridicule. They held her death in the paw. She had no idea. She could feel their shiny button eyes not seeing her and their noses curling in an invasive desire to understand what creature she was and what she was doing. They came into the plot by night and nibbled the seedlings, sat on them and broke them, were repulsed by the pesticidal flavour of the needles.

As long as she was bending and shoving trees into the ground, she was safe. She was touched by the divine and unharmable; she was next to God. But when she came across bear scat, she would lean down to inspect it, looking closely for some sign. She wasn't sure what exactly. She lay down in a bear bed. A clump of thick gold fur clung to a thistle. The smell was between wet dog, damp wool, man stink and fear. Adrenaline gave an edge of excitement, fear shot through her veins and arteries and made her circulatory system alive from heart to cunt. She wanted her lover. She didn't miss him particularly. It was release she was seeking. The insect hum was a natural prayer, incessant.

She put a tree in the ground.

I'm terrified, she said. Two steps and cut a hole, plant, close the gaping hole.

Freak.

The bears were sidling up to each other just out of sight; they were jostling for the wind stream. They wanted the smell coming off her and were nipping each other to catch the whiff. There was an opera of odour to appreciate. The DEET, the perspiration, the perfume, her urine dried on her inner thigh, the crap she couldn't disguise with wiping, which they knew from nuzzling piles of it when she left, and the saliva that smelled of thirst, regurgitated pesticide, anxiety and ingested blackfly all came to the bears in harmony and made some sense of her presence. There were three bears. Three bears to her Goldilocks. They were bachelors and normally wouldn't hang around. If it weren't for Sharon they would have separated long ago. Her odour captivated them.

It rained the second day, a cold inundation that intensified and abated but never ceased. The flies were nevertheless relentless. The rain came down and the blackflies flew up. The chaos of it was hard to stand. Sharon slathered on the Watkins dope and nestled into her slicker. The shovel pried the mud earth open with suction gasps, like mouths. She stuffed the seedlings down in.

At least they get some moisture. Live.

Jeremy was at the tree stash. It was his first year. He was a lank of a boy-man, patchy beard showing pasty skin and pimple craters through its sparsity, someone who spent too much time in libraries and bars, a city punker assuaging parents by getting a good education while walking the fine line of cool. Sharon was half in love with him and half in love with the idea of being half in love with him. He wore a ratty black leather jacket when he wasn't planting, it was buckles all over, innuendo of rough sexual practices. His eyes were an unnatural shade of blue, and standing there with the shovel and tree satchels, he looked for all the world like a spoiled, overgrown elf. She liked the way his pants fit loose, as if held on by sheer will. He was really ugly; she liked that, too.

He said, What do you think, Sharon?

I may die here, she said.

I know what you mean.

The DEET made a chemical reaction with the rubber slicker.

Fumes interfered with her oxygen supply. She took the shortness of breath for anxiety. The bears were watching her. When she came close to the edge of the forest, she strained to see them. She craned her neck and listened to her heart beat twice as fast as it should. She took a step into the woods and heard things.

I'm hearing things, she said to herself. It doesn't matter. They are there or not. It makes exactly no difference. I see them or not.

She yelled, Freak, into the forest and listened as something large lumbered off. She couldn't see anything. She could hear that it was big. Bigger than she was. Maybe there was more than one. Could be a moose. It was as scared of her as she was of it.

Her heart was racing. She took a bundle of black spruce trees out of her bag and stared at it. It looked unfamiliar suddenly. The corridor spun in and out in a confusion of space. Her tree-planting technique was to plant a line down the corridor, the trees sidled up as close as possible to the slash, finding the good micro-site in the ravages left after the scarifier had done its work. At the dead end of the corridor, where the plantable area met the forest, she'd double back and plant her way out. The corridor in which she stood had a wall of debris above her head. She poked around in it as if she was searching for something, as if it could answer some unasked question. She made a small nest inside the debris and placed the bundle of trees in it. She put two more bundles in and pulled the debris back over it. She had finely concealed it. No one would come here with the bear stink and the taste of fear everywhere. No one would ever control this nipple of planted land so close to the edge of the forest. It didn't feel immoral. It felt like nothing.

Sharon leaned into the slash wall and sat into it to rest. The rain had washed the bug dope down her slicker in filthy rivulets. Her long hair was stuck in strings to her cheeks. She had a bundle of trees to plant herself out of the corridor. It was the last outer corridor in the area, and when it was done, she would be planting the inner circlet of winding corridors which spiralled into the centre. The driver had created these spaces as a harassment. Sharon would either have to bag up more trees, double to save time, which was impossible, or she would have to climb over the myriad slash piles again and again to make a straight line back to the tree stash. There was easily another half day's work in the area.

Jeremy! She yelled for him when she got back to the stash.

Yeah, I'm just bagging out. His voice was distant and blurred by the rain.

Sharon squatted by the puddle of trees. The tree runner had found this little cesspool of stagnant water and loaded it with bundles, pressed the roots into the muck and covered the bud unions with sphagnum moss. Sharon reached into the stash, selected twelve bundles and laid them in a pyramid on the ground beside her. The roots dangled longer than the trees. She stood and slapped each bundle on the ground between her legs to drain the water. The seedlings were like sponges, the roots insatiable. She put each root mass under her boot and snapped off the root caps to a manageable length. By then Jeremy had showed up.

I haven't a clue, he said.

No one has, really. Sharon was laughing at him without appearing to.

That new girl? She keeps coming in my area. I ran ticker tape. It should be obvious. It's all fucked up back there now. I keep coming upon her trees and losing direction. It's very weird. I was completely lost for a while, couldn't remember where the tree cache was. Jeremy pulled out a pack of DuMaurier and lit up a smoke, offered Sharon one. They stood there in the rain for some time, smoking and enjoying that.

She's naked from the waist up, got duct tape over her tits, as if it isn't cold or what? Jeremy's cigarette was wet; he was struggling to keep it going, had the Bic going on and off.

Her name is Sarah, said Sharon.

Toshi knows her. She talks to angels. It's Sarah, yeah. Is she stoned?

I don't think so. I've worked with her before, too. She's just like that. You ought to try to ignore her.

Yeah, well, she's got nice tits anyway. There's that at least. Just ignore her.

I can't just ignore her. I don't know. I don't know. She's planting in my corridor.

Blow it off, Jeremy. If she's not in your land, she'll be in someone else's. She's from another planet. Aliens left her here because they couldn't deal with her either. Don't try. It's a waste of time.

I'm earning twenty-five dollars a day before expenses. I'm being eaten alive by insects. Why did I come here?

You're the only one who can answer that, Jeremy.

I wanted a life-altering experience.

That's very funny.

Sharon picked up each bundle of trees and shoved them into her bags. She didn't use the fanny bag except to carry a water bottle. She had to sit on the bag to compress the trees so that she could fit the sixth bundle in each side. Jeremy was staring.

What? she said.

The poor little trees. You're killing them, he said.

I trim them. It disorients them, makes them work harder. They'll grow up to be spindly Northern Ontario swamp trees. Then, when they are harvestable in twenty years, in they come with the feller-buncher to cut them down for arse-wipe. What do you care?

So much for altruism.

Whatever.

He looked like shit, the rain had flattened his punk hairdo so it stuck to the misshapen curve of his skull. His flattened face ran long into his neck. There were smears of muck across his nose and along his mouth where he had wiped insect repellent along with dirt. He was out of place. Like a tall dwarf or an elf. No. More like an enormously tall dwarf. She wanted to climb all over him.

Either way, I feel sorry for the trees, he said.

Sure you do, Jeremy, sure. Well, as they say, the dwarfs are for the dwarfs.

That's very rude of you, he said, before he realized that he'd heard that somewhere before. Was it Narnia? Jeremy looked around him at the decimated landscape, the rape of it, the lack of it, the obscene, wanton, wholesale disregard of it, and he couldn't reconcile it to its past. What did a forest look like, anyway?

I still feel sorry for the trees, he said. I mean they aren't people or anything.

Oh, yes, of course.

Jeremy studied mathematics and classical philosophy. And even though now he balked at the prospect of normalcy, at academic achievement as a representation of worth, at such notions as dressing for success, and even though he played at righteousness vis-à-vis vegetarianism, nihilism (re appearance, re musical tastes), the fact was he was heading toward a long-drawn-out career in corporate accounting. In six years this would all be nostalgia. His entire anti-government, anti-humanity stance would seem quaint and naive. The perspiration that poured off him appeared oily. He watched Sharon pick her way over the slash heap that separated their plots.

He muttered, Thanks for nothing, bitch.

She didn't hear him. The smell rose up to her by the time she got to the top of the heap. She held her shovel aloft and roared to the rain, the atmosphere, the bears. Jeremy looked up in awe. He found her behaviour inscrutable, but what was new? He bagged up two bundles, squinted back into what he believed might be his territory if only Sarah hadn't beaten him to it and headed in. The problem was that Sarah had planted a line of trees diagonally through his area, and whenever he reached it, he would stand there, confused and directionless, glancing here and there for his line of fluttering ticker tape. Finally he cordoned off the plot so that it looked like a crime scene.

Jeremy yanked a tree out of his bag and smoothed the roots into one mass, then he carefully wrapped the tail of the root around the bulk. He stepped on his shovel and wriggled a sodden hole open. He bent and poked the tree into the hole. He pulled himself up and looked around for the next plantable micro-site.

The forest floor was difficult for him to read. What looked like topsoil was airy moss or blackened root mass from a felled tree, or a thin camouflage for the nutritionless sand beneath. He tried spot after spot to no avail and finally grabbed a handful of decayed leaves, placed it roughly six feet from his last tree and cut a hole in the centre of the mass. This took an exhausting ten minutes.

This is insanity, he mumbled. He lunged forward toward the next site and tripped on a thin, snaking root that curled out of the forest floor and back in, like an artery stretched from the body for inspection. Jeremy caught the earth with his mouth and lay there in disbelief until he began to feel comfortable. He got the formula for a polar graph suddenly in his mind and couldn't shake it: $R=4\cos\theta$, a lovely petal-shaped circle graph; he began to colour it in slowly, methodically, in his mind's eye, as one can while falling asleep. The rain drizzled down and dropped off his head to the ground, and he watched as the earth drew in the moisture, mesmerized, until he fell asleep. A search party was sent into his area at the end of the day. He was shaken awake.

Oh, yes, I see, was the first thing he said before he came fully awake. They were relieved that the bears hadn't mauled him. He hadn't answered when they called for him; hours had passed. Sharon's story had exacerbated their concerns.

The three young males heard Sharon roar. They quit foraging and put their noses to the wind. The rain was coming down thickly, interfering with the stream of odour for which they were longing. The roar worried them. What was this creature? She was mostly quiet, bending, rising in a wave of scent that enticed and perplexed them. Now she roars. The insects buzzed around them, they swatted at them and shook them away; they settled immediately along the mucous membranes and fed. The bears followed her winding trail as best they could as she made tighter and tighter turns into the deforested landscape.

Sharon was running with the last trees. She was convinced that no one would ever bother to check the quality of her work; the roots were down, that was good enough for her. Moving faster, she found the quality actually rose, the trees went in without a fuss and stood tall. She wanted to get out of there. She was drenched through with sweat and rain. The nettle and fireweed brushed against her, and there was that bear stink again. The labyrinthine swirls made the work extra mindless. She was meditating on the next tree even as she put one in the ground; her eyes were forward, her nostrils keen to the pulse of that bear smell. They were coming nearer. The land was almost fully planted; then she could die.

The big bear was coming closer for a more intimate sniff. He was having trouble following her at the speed she was turning in and in to the centre of the plot. He had fought for the right, jostling, standing and finally growling and biting his superiority. His motivation was stronger, and the smaller males acquiesced. They leaned into a birch tree and witnessed the big bear leave. He found it tedious to climb the slash heaps, preferring instead to follow the flow of the corridors, snuffling at the ground and higher up in the air to assure himself of her whereabouts. She left a trail of small trees behind her, as if to mark territory. What was she?

Sharon spread the last trees out so that she would finish the area, six by six, with the final trees in the bag and come out even. She stretched the spacing to nine feet and then more until, reaching the dead centre of the plot, with all its intricate winding and doubling back and turning, she stood looking at the last tree, planted. She arched her back for a stretch and took a swig of water. She didn't notice the large, tawny bear sniffing at her like crazy until she turned around to leave the land maze.

On all fours he stood about four feet at the shoulder, but erect, vaguely waving his paws, he was eight feet tall. His nose curled into a permanent sniff. It is useless to climb a tree to avoid a black bear. They are climbing adepts. Sharon felt her heart throb into her mouth, she could taste her own blood spilling, and she dropped like a carcass to the forest floor. She held her breath and tried to control the adrenal fear that coursed through her. He'd smell the deceit, he'd recognize the lie; a bear's instinct is his greatest ally.

This was inevitable. The bears are for the bears, she thought, I've been pursued and captured. I'm dead. I'm dying. This is dying.

She could hear the rain fall and the bear sniffing information. Now she was big; now she was small. It took him a while to locate her. She had her arms wrapped around her head, her legs tucked under her. He found her with his nose, then he dropped down to all fours and approached. The smell of wet fur choked her. He nudged her head with his paw. Then nuzzled her. He licked her. She left trees to mark her territory.

Sharon waited for death. The bear began rocking against her, first slowly and then more rapidly. She thought he was trying to turn her over. No, why would he do that? He took a more obvious position, straddling her as he might a female bear, and continued humping her. She recognized that he was mating with her, or trying to, and her second thought, after relief, was embarrassment. There must be some mistake. His thrust was rough, his paws were digging into her shoulders. There would be blood and scars along her back. This rape would mark her for life.

She almost laughed when she thought that. She couldn't feel anything except the violence of his weight as he pushed and pushed. He nipped at her neck. She was invisible beneath his fur.

Would you crush me? she wondered.

He licked her again when he had spent himself. Then he lumbered slowly out of the labyrinth and on past the two smaller bears, who tried to follow but were kept at bay by a warning bark. He walked deeper and deeper into the forest.

Sharon's ribs were bruised from the weight of the beast, and her sense of self was shattered. She didn't give any details about what had happened except to say she had been mauled and had managed to survive. There was no way to describe the incident without seeming ridiculous.

Jeremy had come to her tent that night to talk to her. He wanted to apologize for being asleep. He wanted in some small way to assume responsibility for what had happened to her. He leaned over her and put his hand alongside hers. It was sinewy, with veins evident and blue. He wanted to hold her, but he didn't dare try it. He was really an awfully shy person, once you got to know him. He said, As I lay there, watching the earth suck in the rain, I was amazed. I'd never seen the earth so close up, you see. I saw it in fine detail, the way it ripples and spits, and the little insects that fly there for protection from the rain. That rest did me a world of good.

Sharon didn't really know what to say. It was obvious he was flirting with her or hoping for something out of this exposition. She felt she liked him better when he'd seemed more brutal. She smiled at him, condescending.

A bear licked me today, she said finally.